MW01122623

Double Danish

Contemporary Short Stories from Denmark

Double Danish
Contemporary Short Stories
from Denmark

Selected and translated
by

Per K. Brask

Cormorant Books

The translator wishes to gratefully acknowledge the assistance of the Danish Ministry of Cultural Affairs in Copenhagen.

Published with the assistance of the Manitoba Arts Council.

Cover from a silkscreen by Michel Lancelot entitled *Le couple A*, used with the kind permission of The Canada Council Art Bank.

Printed and bound in Canada.

Published by
Cormorant Books
RR 1
Dunvegan, Ontario
Canada K0C 1J0

Canadian Cataloguing in Publication Data

Main entry under title:
Double Danish

ISBN 0-920953-46-8

    1. Short stories, Danish—Translations into English.
2. Short stories, English—Translations from Danish.
3.. Danish fiction—20th century—Translations into English 4. English fiction—20th century—Translations from Danish. I. Brask, Per K., 1952-   .

PT8024.E5D69 1991   839.8' 13' 0108074   C91-090140-6

To Carol

ACKNOWLEDGEMENTS

I would like to thank Jan and Gary Geddes of Cormorant Books for believing in this project, the authors, all of whom were generous with comments and suggestions, and Kristjana Gunnars for agreeing to write the foreword. In addition, I would like to thank Kate Hegelund of the Danish Cultural Institute and John Christian Jørgensen, literary editor at Politiken, for their helpful suggestions; Inge and Olaf Brask for their assistance in keeping me informed of the writing scene in Denmark, and Carol Matas for critiquing my translations.

P.B.

TABLE OF CONTENTS

INTRODUCTION by Kristjana Gunnars, 8

A HAPPY TIME by Benny Andersen, 14

DO NOT CROSS THE TRACKS by Jytte Borberg, 31

A PLACE TO BE HUMAN by Bo Green Jensen, 43

ONE OF THE LITTLE SAVIOURS by Ulla Ryum, 56

THE LADY by Niels Hav, 63

THE STAIN by Astrid Saalbach, 69

THE LITTLE NEWCOMER by Claes Johansen, 73

THE HEIGHTS OF HAPPINESS by Hanne Marie Svendsen, 79

ON THE WAY TO THE CEMETERY by Svend Åge Madsen, 85

TO WISH FOR SUDDEN CHANGE by Dorrit Willumsen, 105

NOTES ON THE AUTHORS, 117

INTRODUCTION

Kristjana Gunnars

This collection of contemporary short stories from Denmark is not simply a random gathering of chance takes, placed under one cover because they happen to be Danish. There is a theme to this book and there is a focus in the selection of stories. Broadly put, the focus is on the life of the mind in a modern European, urban, domestic environment. The theme that runs through all the stories is the psychological landscape of a nation of people that appears to have lost its identity, who live in overcrowded settings and scrambled family scenarios where loyalty still holds but the reason for it is blurred.

Most of the authors represented in this volume are dramatists as well as story writers. That observation may go a long way in explaining the elements of psychodrama and theatricality that appear. The playwright's touch may also clarify the absence of settings and landscapes. The focus in all the stories is almost exclusively on the dislocated sensibilities of people who cannot quite understand what is going on, but no matter how absurd those events are, think nothing of it. There is an acceptance of the bizarre which borders on the surrealistic. The whole book plays out its authors' perceived variations of craziness that are contained in modern daily life.

In Benny Andersen's "A Happy Time," the bizarre and the crazy are located in family life. The whole story is acted out on the stage of the family home. Two people marry and live their lives together, raising children and going about their business, while embroiling themselves deeper and deeper in the twisted undercurrents of the unresolved resentments and competitive emotional score keeping. The outsider, a writer who visits them, is both fascinated and repulsed by what appears to be a form of normality that only looks strange from the outside.

In Jytte Borberg's "Do Not Cross the Tracks," the bizarre is to be found in the construction of modern life itself. The isolation of the urban environment where people find themselves so alone they lose all direction is part of that construction. The need to seek out other people while not wanting to involved with them is another. The way apartment dwellings are designed, with the isolation of its compartments and the unnaturalness of the group that is thrown together just because they occupy the same building, is a third. The protagonist appears quite crazy, but as is often the case, it takes a bit of insanity to see things clearly.

Bo Green Jensen's "A Place to Be Human," locates the bizarre in the rootlessness of modern life. We follow a couple on their journey in New Orleans, after spending some time here and there in the United States. The two protagonists are completely seduced by the tourist culture and end up paying all their attention to the crass, absurd, tinselly items of the tourist trade, and no attention at all to the reality of the place they are in. The travellers are living in a kind of papier mâché world which is highly bizarre, but as in the other stories, the victims of the tourist trap appear entirely unaware of how dislocated and absurd they are.

It is in Bo Green Jensen's story that we find a most resounding quotation that describes the thrust of the entire book. The passage is another quotation from a book the protagonist is reading, The Fall of the King, which says: "I lost the true Spring of my life in Denmark longing for happiness in foreign lands. But on my travels I did not find that happiness, for everywhere I longed for my native hearth. And when all the world finally could tempt me no more, then Denmark too had died in my heart and I became homeless."

Story after story plays out the variations of what is contained in that statement. People continually long for something else, so they spend their lives searching for that something else only to discover what they wanted was what they had in the first place. Returning to retrieve it, they find it is no longer there. This would be an encapsulation of the malaise of modernity itself, where we find reconstructions of old time villages and the trade in antiques, which people cling to in the hopes of rediscovering lost ways of life. But those ways of life are gone and are unrecoverable.

In Ulla Ryum's story "One of the little Saviours," the bizarre is something that comes with destiny. What happens to people seems to happen by chance, and looks like an accident to them. But seen from a larger perspective, there is a synchronicity of chance that bears out the suspicion that instead of a universe of meaning, we have a universe of irony. The irony that is played out, of which we are the pawns, is, to use Margaret Lawrence's phrase, a kind of cruel "Jest of God." It is not so much we who are crazy, as the other authors might suggest, or even the world we have constructed for ourselves to live in, but destiny itself that designs ironies at random. We live, in other words, in a bizarre universe.

Niels Hav's "The Lady" offers us another view of the bizarreness of modern urban life and a brutal comment on the isolation we experience as participants in modernity. The crowded city is full of people we do not know. The protagonist is found wandering about purposelessly through an urban panorama which is simply labelled instead of described. He ends up in a cafeteria which is so crowded he has to share a table with a lady he never met before. The two lunch eaters find themselves in a relationship, and the distinguishing factor is the brevity of it. The thing about modern life which is really bizarre, the story seems to contend, is the flash in the pan nature of the relationships we carry out. Unhappily, those instant cash friendships that are acquired and spent in a few moments have to serve in lieu of real relationships, which do not seem to exist.

For Astrid Saalbach in "The Stain," the absurdity is

the way we deny our natures as we go through the motions of our existence. Here we are accurately located, namely in the theatre, which serves as a metaphor for the environment in which we live generally. There follows a highly realistic description of a young actress suffering from menstrual cramps who has to lie down between stage appearances in the leading man's dressing room. But it is not a home, it is a green room. The man is not himself, he is a character in a play. She is not herself, she is another character on a break. All of this simply emphasizes the way most of us feel in everyday life, playing out our parts, trying not to embarrass ourselves. When the young actress finds she has bled through onto the couch, she is embarrassed and humiliated, as if she had done something wrong. There is also the problem of going back on the stage like that. It is bizarre, in other words, that our physicality itself, instead of making us enjoy life, somehow gets in the way.

Claes Johansen gives the idea of the absurdity of our physicality and its place in our lives an entirely unappetizing twist in "The Little Newcomer." This story may be read as a cruel attack on pro abortionists, but on a broader scale it can be seen as a comment on the crazy way we perceive things. A family of four is living a presumably normal existence. The mother, rather unnaturally huge, is pregnant and has a completely painless and surprising miscarriage in the shower. She dumps the foetus in the trash but when the husband asks for it she fishes it out and sets it on the table in the middle of dinner. Readers may find this unacceptably gross, but the story appears to be asking us whether we do not in fact, in real life, do things in relation to nature which are equally gross. We are, ourselves, in the way we treat nature, bizarre people.

Hanne Marie Svendsen in "The Heights of Happiness," locates the bizarre in the way in which we limit our natures. We live in such a restricted way that we deny ourselves the pleasures of life we might have had if we simply gave in. The story is a toast to dancing, more or less, wherein the narrator gives us one reason after another why dancing is such a wonderful thing to do. A fantasy of the Copenhagen Central Station culminates the narrative, where the depot, usually crammed with busy and grim people who have no time to stop and enjoy, and no reason to in that demure station either, suddenly turns into a wonderful Viennese dance hall. The vision presents a graphic description of the absurd self denials of modern life as we rush from one place to another.

Svend Åge Madsen located the bizarre, like Ulla Ryum, in destiny. A cruel twist of fate has a man killed by a passing motorcar. The driver of the car, to assuage his feeling of anxiety and guilt, starts to surround the home and family of the man he has accidentally killed. The dead man had everything the driver, or live man, wanted: a home, a family, a job. As the driver presses into his victim's family, he eventually takes the dead man's place. In a universe of ironies, it is therefore not surprising to find the protagonist is struck by the idea that the fate of the man whose part he is playing is always going to turn out the same. Therefore he himself must be destined to die in a car accident as he crosses the street someday. The vision presented is straight out of The Twilight Zone. The universe itself is bizarre, we are pawns in a "jest of God," and there is not a thing we can do about it.

Dorrit Willumsen's "To Wish for a Sudden Change" locates the absurd in story telling itself. This is a story composed of several small stories, each one different. The reader has to start all over again when entering a new vignette, and there is no continuity between the individual segments. The act of reading and the act of telling the story have developed to a point of craziness. The attention span required for each segment is so short one might think the narrative is constructed in spite of itself. The quick focus of the segments implies a view of the reader as a disinterested and scattered being who has just about no time for an extended narrative. Inside this structure, however, there is a repeated sensation in segment after segment, that the fictional characters portrayed are caught in traps they wish to get out of but lack the ability to articulate, even emotionally, that desire. The characters do, in fact, "wish for a sudden change," but the bizarreness of it is that they hardly seem to know it.

All together, the stories in this collection portray a remarkable sense of emptiness. It is as if the contents of civilized community life had all been emptied out and what is left is a skeleton of structures through which people aimlessly amble and the wind cruelly blows. There seems to have been a psychological flood which has washed everything we know and relied on away. What we are left with is a kind of post-nuclear existence, emotionally. We are in the wake of the devastation of modernity, where even sanity appears to have departed. Or perhaps there is no such thing as sanity. The moment witnessed by these stories is the very moment portrayed in one of the Twilight Zone stories—since the analogy has been made already once.

A man who loves to read is not allowed to by his family and boss. To read, he locks himself up in a bank vault during his lunch hour. On one of these lunch breaks a nuclear bomb is detonated. When he emerges everyone is gone and only buildings and their contents remain. To his happiness he discovers the New York Public Library and millions of books everywhere. Now, he thinks, he finally has peace to read. He piles up all the books and sits down to start a lifetime of reading. When he bends down to pick up the first book, his glasses fall off his face and break.

Happy reading.

A HAPPY TIME

Benny Andersen

On a reading tour I stayed overnight with some old friends who had moved to one of the larger cities in the provinces. I gave a reading at the central library and the next morning I went for a walk in the neighbourhood before lunch, after which I was to take the train north. On a tour like this around the country you spend a lot of time in various train compartments so I usually take advantage of every opportunity to stretch my legs and have a look around.

This was a residential neighbourhood with older houses, a few three story apartment blocks, a super market, a hair dresser's salon, a newspaper kiosk, a bakery. It dawned on me that I had lived here once, in the beginning of the Fifties, when I was a touring musician. Back then the neighbourhood was quite new and at the edge of town. The outskirts were now considerably further out. Sometimes it can be hard to recognize an old acquaintance who's grown a beard since you last saw him. Now, you could barely see the houses behind trees and bushes. Back then the neighbourhood was bright and transparent. You had to be careful not to step on newly-planted trees and bushes, naked twigs stuck into the ground. They looked helpless and, as if blinded by the sunshine, they reached out with a few fumbling side shoots in an attempt to figure out where they were. Now, thirty years later, they didn't doubt for a moment that they were the ones protecting the houses under their sheltering wings in the form of weeping birches, larch trees, acacia trees, or, that they, in the form of hedges of hornbeam, barberry, privet or whitethorn, were responsible for keeping curious passers-by at an appropriate distance.

The neighbourhood seemed both recognizable and unrecognizable to me. I tried to recall street names but I couldn't recall the name of the street I used to live on till I suddenly saw the sign; Oluf's Alle. At the same moment I remember that it was in number seventeen that I had stayed for a month or so back in 1951. The name of my former hosts was Jacobsen with a "c", rather than the usual "k".

I went down the street on the sidewalk, which was gravel back then, but now flagged, till I reached number seventeen where I had to concentrate in order to recognize the place. The low bungalow in yellow brick was just visible between the branches in the foreground. In the middle of the front yard stood an enormous weeping willow whose sad-looking crown hang so far down over the sidewalk you had to separate its soft braids with your hands.

To the right of the weeping willow stood two spruce trees and another two stood to the left of it. The two closest to the willow were short and crooked. Every second twig was dry and naked, every other one was stretched out in what looked like a twisted desperate hand gesture. The two furthest from the willow were towering majestically, their trunks naked to the midpoint, while their upper layers of branches attempted in a swaying, admonishing movement to stand against gusts of wind which could not be felt down here on the ground. But a flurry from my youth began to move the twigs and branches of my memory. I was twenty-two years-old back then, searching and insecure, but with a hunger for life. The Jacobsens were in their late thirties and as far as I could tell they had a horrible time together.

Through a rental agency I had rented a room for a month in Professor and Mrs. Jacobsen's newly built yellow brick house. At the edge of the new lawn of the front yard stood eight small Christmas trees and a yellow limp twig supported by a bamboo stick, the unimpressive overture to the now so luxurious weeping willow.

Everything in the house was shiny and new, and everything was in its proper place, nothing was allowed to be messy. A piece of paper falling over the edge of the table never touched the floor before a couple of the inhabitants smashed their heads together in an attempt to catch it. A fingerprint on a glass resulted in the glass being washed several times in steaming hot water. A speck of birdshit on a window was barely noticed before the window cleaner was called to clean all of the windows inside and out.

The same applied to the inhabitants. Both Mr. and Mrs. Jacobsen and their two children of seven and eleven were well-groomed and well-dressed morning and night. Mr. Jacobsen was tall, with dark hair and broad shoulders. Mrs. Jacobsen was tall, blond and slim. They looked more like a lawyer couple in a Hollywood movie than they did a Danish professor and a public school teacher. They never touched each other when I was around, and when they touched their children they were careful not to crumple their clothes or mess their hair.

It soon dawned on me that all this neatness wasn't so much the result of a genetic predisposition or of a learned sense of order and cleanliness as it was a safeguard, a barricade, designed to expose the fewest possible vulnerable points. In my youthful naïvete I thought at first that possible attackers or critics had to be expected from the outside: neighbours, family, visitors, but I quickly realized that it was Mr. and Mrs. Jacobsen who were each other's opponents and vigilant critics.

As a piano player in a bar I went to bed late and had no need of feeling obliged to join the family for an early breakfast before they dispersed to various educational institutions. Mrs. Jacobsen offered to leave some coffee for me in a thermos and to leave me an egg covered in potholders and a tea warmer. But a strange need drove me to get up early and join them for breakfast after which I would go back to bed when they had all left the house. Perhaps it was a feeling that my presence would make them control themselves so that they at least wouldn't physically attack each other. Perhaps it arose from a vague hope that one morning their subtle disagreements would vanish in a liberating laughter and that the whole thing would prove to be a devilish game instigated only to fool and frighten their young, naïve lodger. But mainly I think I was driven by fascination, my curiosity to witness what they would do next to surpass each other at inventive, verbal terror.

Slowly I discovered there were game rules which had to be kept. They never attacked each other directly, personally. Probably their perfection in dress and their neatness were the results of an earlier phase in their relationship during which they had criticized each other on those points. A phase during which their battles had been more primitive and fought more directly. But they had left this stage behind long ago. Now, there was nothing to find fault with—even the eggs were perfectly boiled. Mr. Jacobsen's was soft boiled, Mrs. Jacobsen's was medium and the children's eggs were just a tad more well done. As I didn't have any particular preference my eggs were alternately soft boiled, medium and hard boiled, and fried eggs on Sundays. Everyone cracked open their egg at the same time, took a couple of mouthfuls, and then the game could begin.

Mr. Jacobsen leaned back and dried his chin with his serviette though there wasn't the smallest hint of a yellow drop on his masculine film star jaw. But perhaps this was a gesture left over from a time when his wife had criticised him for having egg yolk dripping from the corners of his mouth? Mrs. Jacobsen picked up her serviette, cast a glance at it and put it back with a satisfied expression revealing that she had no need at all for a serviette. She had a gorgeous, slightly oriental face with tall, slanted cheekbones and eyes like an Egyptian queen—except that they were blue. Her nose was narrow and arched slightly. She looked around, turning her head in sudden, jerky movements like a rare, long-necked breed of chicken. Having registered that everything was as it should be she could say something like: "Isn't it a little on the cool side in here?"

The children put down their egg spoons silently and looked attentively at one, then the other, of their parents. They hadn't used their serviettes. In fact, apart from Mr. Jacobsen's serviette I never saw any of them in use. His seemed for some reason or other to have attained the status of a special introductory prop. I didn't dare use my serviette. Instead, I would cheat by using my handkerchief if ever something slipped out through my gaping mouth.

"It feels too hot for me," said Mr. Jacobsen loosening his tie.

"Pia, would you please bring mommy's blue shawl," Mrs. Jacobsen said. And while Pia rushed to get the shawl, Mr. Jacobsen took off his jacket and hung it on the back of his chair. Mrs. Jacobsen grabbed on to her coffee cup with both hands and shivered. Mr. Jacobsen picked up his serviette and began to fan himself with it.

"It's going to be a scorcher," he groaned.

Pia came back with the shawl. Mrs. Jacobsen wrapped herself in it and stuck a shivering hand out from under it.

"Look Pia, mommy has goose bumps! Remember to put on your scarf before you go to school. We don't want you catching a cold again!"

Mr. Jacobsen wiped his forehead with his serviette. I don't know how he did it but one large, visible drop of sweat succeeded another and his serviette was soon drenched and crumpled up. He reached for his son's serviette:

"Let me have yours, Rasmus."

"Your hands are always so nice and warm, Pia!" Mrs. Jacobsen said. "Would you please hold my fingers till they're warm?"

"Could you open a window, Rasmus?" Mr. Jacobsen said.

"Oh no, it's already seven thirty. I won't have time

for a hot bath," Mrs. Jacobsen whimpered.

"At least I'll have to change my shirt and vest," Mr. Jacobsen said. "This is simply too much..."

Everyone rose from the table. Five minutes later they'd all left the house and I went back to bed without really knowing whether I was too cold or too hot and not really being able to fall asleep till a quarter of an hour into the afternoon just as they all returned one after the other slamming the door behind them as if they were being chased.

By then it was time for me to get up and get ready, get washed and shaved before walking downtown where I was performing. Already back then I loved to walk and I had a dream of being able to sneak out unseen, walk into town, go into a few shops, buy a newspaper, a new comb, a packet of cough drops and things like that. Then around six o'clock I would sit down calmly in a small, cosy restaurant and spend an hour or so without company other than my own, a sumptuous meal, half a bottle of red wine, the newspaper and the shadow of a waiter, until shortly before eight when I could sit down at the piano in the lounge across the street feeling full, slightly tipsy and relaxed. Just for one single day. It would not only have been wonderful it would also have been appropriate since my rent expressly included only breakfast. But shortly before 5 p.m., no matter how carefully I tried to slip away on my silent rubber soles I was stopped and seduced by Mrs. Jacobsen standing in the doorway to the kitchen.

"You're not leaving already, are you Mr. Andersen? We're having sirloin steak and new potatoes sprinkled with fresh parsley from the garden for dinner. I've got plenty and I am certain that you won't find a better meal in any of the restaurants in this town anyway."

Mrs. Jacobsen's eyes were large and bright as she looked back and forth at me and the still closed front door with these jerky movements which had a hypnotic effect. My stuttering attempts at explaining that I didn't want to cause any inconvenience were quickly brushed aside by her tinkling laughter, and since these were the only moments I saw her smile and laugh I gave in without further resistance. Mumbling, I made polite noises of gratitude while inside I felt a peculiar sense of shame as if I had given in to a nefarious but irresistible vice.

Even though I must admit that the food was always delicious and perfectly prepared I was incapable of enjoying it. I was unable to concentrate on what I was eating because of the ritual game I'd become an involuntary witness to. Actually, I only recall the parsley. There was always freshly cut parsley sprinkled atop the potatoes, the wedges of tomato or the fillets of fish. For many years after I would shiver whenever anybody mentioned the word parsley.

One day I changed my strategy. Instead of sneaking to the front door I got there in three bouncing steps and pulled open the door only to end up standing face to face with Mr. Jacobsen who stood there with a bunch of freshly cut parsley which, smiling, he slowly lifted up to my nose so I could attest to its undeniable freshness. He must have picked it in the back garden but still he came in through the front door with it. I retreated backwards into the foyer while Mr. Jacobsen followed with his parsley challenge kept at a constant two centimetres from my nose. After this I abandoned my new strategy.

Soon after we were gathered around the dinner table again: sirloin steak, chicken, sausage, pork, flounder, or whatever, something or other with parsley sprinkled on it.

The game could begin. Somebody had to break the silence. Who would it be today? Was there an order to whose turn it was? I was careful not to be the one, but sometimes it was one of the children who could exclaim something like:

"Look, my potato has a funny nose!"

I noticed in situations like that that the Jacobsens, who usually avoided looking directly at each other, would cast a rapid glance at each other. It was only a matter of a split second but it was evidently sufficient to decide who would start because they never spoke simultaneously nor did they interrupt each other. It was as if they found the very possibility of their sentences overlapping so humiliating that they always let the other complete a statement.

"It looks like a sculpture. A Picasso or an Arp!" Mr. Jacobsen said.

"I just wish modern artists weren't so intent on distorting reality," Mrs. Jacobsen said. "Why can't art simply look like what it is supposed to represent? But evidently there are forces striving with all their power to simplify and debase everything!"

Pia, who had just bitten the nose off her potato, carefully put the rest of it back onto her plate while she almost imperceptibly chewed on the nose with her back molars.

"The most important exponents of modern art see it as their task to liberate in us that which is our most fundamental human essence," Mr. Jacobsen said.

"But what they manage to lay before us is sickness and rot," Mrs. Jacobsen replied while Pia carefully spat out the rest of the potato onto her fork held behind her serviette.

"They liberate a malignant tumour but the individual dies!"

"Wasn't it Hitler who spoke about *Entartet Kunst*," Mr. Jacobsen smiled cruelly, and I thought, "Touché!" But Mrs. Jacobsen replied with such speed that only later was I able to recognize how cleverly she had exposed this blunder:

"Herr Hitler was after all a very mixed-up person surrounded by confused advisors. Modern art is not at all degenerate, but rather, it is childish in its pursuit of the primitive, the uncultured, the simple. Picasso, Arp, and whoever they are, people from the twentieth century's highly cultivated Europe who with all devilish intent want to imitate primitive African art. It is just too silly for

—21—

words!"

Mr. Jacobsen had guided a piece of food on his fork all the way into his mouth before he moved it out a few centimetres and said casually: "There are those who'd claim that much of African art is very highly developed, even refined."

"I have no doubt that there are people like that!" Mrs. Jacobsen exclaimed with a snappy turn of her head to the side and back again.

And that's how it went. Not just through this meal, but day after day. The themes would change from meal to meal and if earlier themes were taken up again they were treated in new and surprising ways. What I found most fascinating was probably the untiring inventiveness, the amazing improvisational flair with which they managed to vary and expand on themes. On one hand it looked as if their marriage had stagnated but on the other hand there was something almost dynamic about the way it had stagnated. They hadn't become indifferent to each other; in a negative way they were totally absorbed in each other. The rest of us were merely spectators or at the most super-numeraries and property staff who silently had to watch the two lead actors as they hatefully circled around each other or around the deep, still fuming crater their love had left behind.

I was never able to discern any concrete reason for their plight. As far as I could tell there were no affairs, no alcoholism, no economic hardship nor any trouble with their jobs. They were relatively young, good-looking, well-to-do and intelligent, had apparently every possibility of living an exuberant and harmonic family life together in our small, relatively well-to-do country which was moving towards better times.

My initial vague conjectures of them putting on a play in my honour to confuse me were slowly being put to shame.

Only on the last day of my stay did I obtain a kind of

certainty that their so eagerly maintained misalliance was the dark side of a love which for some reason had become impossible.

I wanted to take the street car to the train station but Mr. Jacobsen insisted on paying for a taxi and for once Mrs. Jacobsen agreed with him.

"You've been a very good lodger, Mr. Andersen, perhaps you could send us a postcard now and then?"

"Don't pester Mr. Andersen," Mr. Jacobsen said, smiling. "You want him to send us a postcard both now and then. Really, then alone would be plenty!"

To my surprise Mrs. Jacobsen couldn't help but smile at Mr. Jacobsen's slim joke so I quickly joined in the laughter. Mr. Jacobsen placed my light suitcase just inside the gate and while we waited for the taxi we inspected the young plants in the front garden. Though it was larger than the back garden it really only consisted of a lawn with a birdbath placed on it. At the edges of the lawn stood a few small bushes or bushes-to-be. Against the house stood a row of crooked sticks, the red thorns on which proclaimed that future summers would see the splendour of roses. But along the white picket fence facing the yellow gravel sidewalk stood the eight small spruce and a weakling of a twig tied to a bamboo stick. I was careless enough to ask Mr. Jacobsen what it was.

"That's supposed to become a weeping willow, Andersen. It's hard to tell now and perhaps we'll never get to see it. Before long the spruce trees will grow well beyond it and kill it in their shadow," Mr. Jacobsen said.

I was just about to ask him why they'd planted them so close together then, but I stopped myself.

"It is well known that willows are extremely greedy for water," Mrs. Jacobsen explained, "especially weeping willows. That's why you usually find them on the banks of a lake where they belong."

"As spruce belong in a spruce forest," Mr. Jacobsen said.

"In a matter of a few years this little twig of a willow will be able to dry out the entire garden until everything withers, and those small spruce will at best be allowed to grow mangled," Mrs. Jacobsen said, her voice tinged with melancholy.

"Time will tell," Mr. Jacobsen said quietly and Mrs. Jacobsen repeated tearfully, "Yes, time will tell."

This moment of my departure was the first time I had heard this couple become close to something that resembled an agreement. What surprised me just as much was that they didn't go on; that they stopped there.

It was a spring morning and the sun was shining, but still there was a veil of haze enveloping a couple of tall trees on the undeveloped lot across the street. You could hear a black bird in the back garden and little farther away the twitter of a chaffinch and a great tit. It was one of these mornings when you can't tell whether the day will turn warm or cold. A large, red earthworm slithered through the short, wet grass right in front of my newly polished brown shoes. Somewhere close by I heard the deep hum of a bumble bee, but I couldn't see it. Instead I happened to see Mrs. Jacobsen wipe a tear from one of her high cheek bones.

Mr. Jacobsen cleared his throat a couple of times.

"Sooo—," he began, stopped and got lost in his own thoughts. A little later he continued, "If ever you should happen to pass this way..."

None of us had heard the taxi approach but suddenly it stopped in front of the house and the driver came up to the gate. Relieved, we said goodbye and as I waved from the passenger seat I felt that I had reached safety. I felt intoxicated with relief and I kept gabbing to the driver about all sorts of things on our way downtown. One thought was crystal clear to me: whatever happened to me in the future I would never come this way again!

But now I had, more than thirty years later. And even though I had experienced a bit of everything during my time as a touring musician and later on as a writer, seeing this place again produced in me the stirring of an almost forgotten sense of discomfort, the painful, powerless sense of being embarrassed on someone else's behalf.

It was the same time of year as back then but a little later in the day and it was cloudy; it could begin to rain at any moment. Nothing was as it once had been. The weeping willow had won, there were only four spruce left and the two that stood closest to the willow were not doing too well. For a moment I wondered what had happened to the Jacobsens. Perhaps they'd kept their game going for another dozen years, maybe less, until their children grew up, and they probably didn't live there any longer.

I was sheltered by the large crown of the weeping willow but I could sense the smell of the earth after the first few raindrops and I was about to pull out of my reverie when I heard a voice behind me.

"Excuse me. Can I help you?"

I turned around and saw a tall, elderly gentleman with a reddish, chiselled face below his white combed back hair. He was holding a worn, brown attaché case close to his long cotton coat, and at the sight of my face he almost dropped it.

"But it's you, Mr. Andersen. What a surprise. We've been following your career from afar. What a pleasure. What brings you to town?"

He put his case under his left arm so he could offer me his hand and I heard a low, muffled clinking sound as if from bottles wrapped in thin paper. I sensed his sweet and sour breath but I wasn't close enough to determine whether it had been produced by a heavy lager or by a stout. As he talked I noticed that the left corner of his mouth was crooked and downwards drawn. In fact, the entire left side of his face seemed immobile, presumably the result of a small stroke. He halted slightly on his left leg as we approached the house.

"Please, do come in for a moment, Mr. Andersen. I

realize that you're probably busy but my wife would never forgive me if she didn't get to see you!"

"But ... You see ... My train ..."

My weak protestations were not only lost on him but also on myself who once again let myself be seduced to go inside this painful place.

The interior of the house no longer smelled of ammonium and cleaning powder as in the old days, but of dust and mould. And because of the trees the rooms were much darker than I remembered. But I recognized Mrs. Jacobsen right away despite the fact that she looked even more haggard and aged than her husband. The beautiful slight slant her eyes used to have had reversed and they were pulled down into a pair of flabby bags of skin which seemed to droop down well below her jaw line. But her jerky, chicken-like head movements, turning first her left eye, then her right one towards us, were exactly as I remembered. She sat in a wheelchair, one arm in a sling and one foot in a cast. The bags around her jaw quivered as she leaned forward and yelled, "Where have you been?"

"Look who's come to see you, my dear. It's Mr. Andersen who lived with us in, in..."

"Fifty-one," I interjected.

"Anybody can show up and say that," she interrupted. "You know I'm almost blind and you take advantage of that and bring home your drinking buddies!"

"But surely you recognize Mr. Andersen. He's a well known..."

"I don't know anybody, and I don't want to know anybody else. I'm fed up with knowing people thank you very much!"

I intimated to Mr. Jacobsen that I would leave but he took me by the arm and pulled me closer to the wheelchair.

"You could at least say hello, my dear!"

"You could at least let me sit here and rot in peace!" she hissed. Then she suddenly opened her eyes as wide as the bags under them would allow and turned one piercing eye towards me, winked grotesquely and screamed in a loud parrot-like voice, "Hello, hello, hello!"

"Hello," I managed to mumble.

She slumped back in her chair and closed her eyes. "There. Now can I be allowed to die in peace?"

Mr. Jacobsen let go of my arm, made a fist with his hand and stamped one foot onto the floor so hard he almost lost his balance and had to hold onto me again.

"That's it, isn't it!" he yelled. "All you want is to die before I do!"

Without opening her eyes, she said, "You're a fool."

"You're my witness, Mr. Andersen! This is the thanks I get for caring for her instead of sending her to a home where she belongs!"

"Care for!" Mrs. Jacobsen's voice grew and she opened one eyelid. "You only care for yourself! You drift about in the street without your cane—knowing full well that at any moment you can trip and tumble into the gutter again with another stroke," and then she made the sound of an ambulance.

"That's a lie!" He gasped and held onto his head.

"You're the one doing everything possible to die before me, so I can be left here totally helpless!" she said.

"That's a complete distortion of the truth," he whined. "Weren't you the one who fell down the stairs?"

"Exactly! And who could have prevented that? Who had left me alone?"

"I was out shopping!"

"Beer and schnapps!"

"Ground veal! And Mazarin cakes, delicious Mazarin cakes for you!"

"And schnapps."

"No, buttermilk! You love buttermilk!"

"What has that to do with anything? Besides it doesn't take hours to buy buttermilk!"

"I was gone for half an hour at the most. Not even that. I appeal to you as an impartial witness to this dispute,

Mr. Andersen, but the fact is—as you've probably been able to ascertain so far—that my wife knows very well how much she means to me and she takes advantage of that—by falling down the stairs to the basement for example in the hope that I'll find her dead when I return..."

"And you who, drunk out of you skull, rush into the worst traffic everyday in the hope that your brain will blow up completely, leaving me here to die of hunger and thirst!"

"You don't know what you're saying!" Mr. Jacobsen screamed foaming at the corners of his mouth. "Mr. Andersen, you are my witness, listen to me, look at me. Do I look like I'm crazy?"

The question confused me and since he in fact did look quite crazy with his bristling white hair, his eyes rolling wildly and his twisted, foaming mouth I almost answered yes, but I managed to stutter, "Not-not-not at all!"

"Did you hear that? Did you hear that?" He screamed insanely, flailing his arms. He turned back towards me again and continued in a more controlled manner.

"I'm glad you came, Mr. Andersen. It's too bad you can't stay longer. But, I don't see anybody but my wife in this vale of tears. We never see the children. Pia is married and living in Australia, Rasmus is fishing salmon in Alaska. That's the thanks you get for putting children on the earth. And here am I an old wreck with a wife who tries to drive me insane. But you know the worst of it, Mr. Andersen?"

He grabbed onto my jacket with both hands and pulled me so close to his face that I could see every little broken vessel branching into his dulled, white eyeballs.

"The worst of it is," he whispered, "that she refuses to believe that I love her—that I love her so much that it hurts right here..."

He let go of my jacket and grabbed at his heart with a heaving sigh.

"Well, now he's once again trying to find some excuse for dying right in front of my eyes!" Mrs. Jacobsen exclaimed putting forward first her right eye, then her left. Mr. Jacobsen, delighted, winked at me.

"That's a good one. One minute she can't see the tip of her own nose; the next she can see anything she wants!"

"Now it's your heart, tomorrow it's your brain, the day after God only knows what!" She complained. "That's what he thinks love is. It's like trying to teach a monkey to play the violin! How could he ever understand the love of a woman? I have sacrificed everything, everything and he thinks he can repay me with a snap of his fingers, by keeling over with a heart attack or by splattering down into the nearest gutter with a stroke. He's a fool and he's made a fool out of me..."

Without asking permission I went to the phone and called a cab.

Mr. Jacobsen followed me to the door as his wife yelled her objections. "You're not drifting about any more today! You'd better keep yourself alive the last few weeks I have left!"

The rain had passed over and I took a couple of deep breaths of the fresh humid Spring air, listened to the amazing rolls of jubilation coming from the black bird in the back garden, and the great tit and the chaffinch. The bumble bee was missing, but instead I heard a series of drum solos produced by a woodpecker working away at a telephone pole across the street. Much had changed, some things were the same, but at least life continued out here. When my taxi arrived I became so happy it almost brought tears to my eyes. Again, I felt this joy, this intoxicating relief at escaping, grateful to be alive and, I hoped, with still quite a lot of life ahead of me. And again, I felt this need to talk. I wanted to say something about how they, after all, had come closer to each other, that they no longer talked past each other, that from my perspective they seemed closely knit, and that this after all was preferable to the painful, icy, hateful atmosphere I remembered from fifty-one, but I wasn't able to turn my phrases so that they would not appear tactless or wounding. The driver was parked at the curb, his meter ticking so I just mumbled, 'Well, good-bye and thank you. It'll probably be a while before I come back through town ..."

Mr. Jacobsen grabbed both my hands and pressed them against his heart.

"You're always welcome here, Mr. Andersen. And don't worry about us!"

"Uhm—I uh ..." I didn't know what to say.

"Because, you see. Nobody and nothing can ever take away from us the good years we had together!"

"Uh, what do you mean?"

He smiled in a friendly manner and let go of my hands and despite the many wrinkles around his eyes they took on a youthful, lively gleam.

"You know very well what I mean, Mr. Andersen. What cheers me up when things get rough are my memories from back then. Back when you stayed with us. We'd only lived here half a year, the house was new, the children were still in school, we were together, we were a family! My wife and I were young and we had many years ahead of us, lots of possibilities, young and healthy. We had the strength back then, Mr. Andersen, the strength to get on with life— those were our good years, it was a happy time. And even though I know it will never return it is my memories of it which hold me up when times are hard. No one can ever take that time away from me! But I won't keep you. I wish you all possible happiness for the future..."

I got into the cab and luckily my driver this time was very talkative and entertaining so all I had to do was nod and grunt every once in a while. I was incapable of talking about the weather, the price of gas, foreign workers, the results of the pools or whatever else one talks about sitting next to the driver. He probably entertained me with issues like that but I don't remember. I probably wasn't listening.

DO NOT CROSS THE TRACKS

Jytte Borberg

There's a knock on the front door. He gets up and quietly he sneaks out through the back door and down the back-stairs in order to get to the backyard.

He rarely takes this route when he leaves his apartment. He hates the narrow staircase with its food odour and all the junk people leave out here because they don't have room for it in their apartments. He has to edge his way through to get to the backyard which consists of a slab of grey cement and a few stair wells leading down to the basement bicycle hold.

The tenants ought to do something to get a proper yard. At least the children would have a decent play-ground then. Maybe it would even make it possible for the adults to get to know each other. They could have picnics there during the summer months. The backyard is the only place where that would be possible because on the front stairs you only meet your neighbour walking to and from the garbage chute or the elevator. Once on the sidewalk everyone turns into anonymous passers-by.

When he reaches the backyard he stands still for only the couple of seconds it takes him to decide which direction to take.

He chooses the gate leading to a labyrinth of small, narrow alleys. The old part of town. The other gate leads to a park which could have provided a place for the chil-dren to play but it is notorious for muggings and people on the make. Most parents consequently forbid their children to go there.

He chooses the alleys not because he wants to stay

anonymous, for everybody is anonymous no matter where they are, but because he's convinced himself that he likes bricks better than trees, the grey cement squares of the sidewalk better than green lawns, that he is better able to breathe in the narrow streets than he is in open parks.

In the alleys he drifts about and turns down every new corner. He walks in a circle, he zigzags and he's so calm and relaxed that he even takes time to nod to some of the shoppers.

After he's drifted about in this well-known part of town for a while he leaves it for the newer neighbourhoods.

Soon everything seems so different to him that both the people and the houses appear to him to be more disintegrated, more cheerless and more monotonous than those in the old part of town. At first this seems strange to him. After all, this is supposed to be new. Then he becomes frightened, but he doesn't know of what. Perhaps he's afraid of getting lost. But, is that possible without a destination? A dog follows him. It barks at him till it reaches the end of the territory it's supposed to protect after which it continues joyfully trotting along a few feet behind him.

He turns around and looks at it disapprovingly. It wags its tail. He tells it to go to hell. He yells, rages and threatens it. It wags its tail. He walks on as if the dog wasn't there and soon it runs up beside him and looks at him with a newly-found sense of submission gleaming in its eyes. He sneaks into the entrance to an apartment block and stays there till he feels certain that the dog has left.

When he comes back out the dog even has the gall to display its happiness at seeing him again. His memory of the persistent knocking on his door mixes with his irritation at the persistent dog. He kicks an empty pail of paint clattering into the gutter.

This morning his shoes were freshly polished. Now they are covered in grey dust. It must have been a long time since it rained. If he could find a store specializing in rain clothes they'd be able to tell him exactly how long it's been since it rained. But there are no specialty stores in a neighbourhood like this. He accepts the dust on his shoes and thinks that if he were to pat the dog it too would probably prove very dusty. He doesn't pat it. He wouldn't dream of it. He doesn't talk to it; he doesn't even look at it and he hopes that soon it will realize just how unwanted it is.

Close by a voice thanks him. True to habit he must have put a coin into an outstretched hand. He likes doing that because it gives him a pleasant feeling of having helped someone without further obligation. But he doesn't get away with it so easily this time for it seems that the outstretched hand is following him. A figure, an old, weak woman, has gotten up from the sidewalk. She looks like an amorphous bundle of clothes trying to keep itself together with a huge, carpet-like, cobalt blue shawl. Her eyes have the same expression as the dog's.

He spits on the sidewalk and he doesn't turn around again. Behind him he can hear the dog and the woman fighting to be in the lead.

By the time it begins to grow dark he's both hungry and tired. By then he has reached the very edge of the city. Here he chooses a house at random and walks in to find out where it might be possible to find a place to sleep. The people there suggest that he go into town where they have hotels in all kinds of price ranges. Patiently he explains to the people that he just came from there and that he has no desire to go back. Hesitantly, they give him the addresses of a couple of hookers adding that in all likelihood they aren't home because they too go downtown to look for action. That's where everything happens, they tell him.

As predicted no one is home at the first address. But at the next one a girl opens the door, points angrily at the dog and the bundle of cobalt blue cloth, and asks if he intends that they come in too. He assures her that he doesn't even know them and he is let in. She wants her payment before showing him the room. She speaks in a hard and abrupt manner but after he's paid twice as much as she asked for, her voice settles into a somewhat softer pitch. She even puts a new sheet on the bed before she leaves.

Though he is hungry he falls asleep immediately and he doesn't wake up until she returns. Tired and quiet.

He sits up in bed leaning against the pillow and asks if there's any chance of a cup of coffee. Yes, there is if he goes down to the lounge on the corner, she answers sullenly, but then she explains why she doesn't feel like making coffee: it's been hard for her to be without her room. She had to make use of backbreaking car seats, find shelter in cold portals, under horrible stair wells and in public wash-rooms.

He tells her that he paid her amply enough for the room for her to take the night off. She doesn't respond to that but tells him instead that those two are still out there. Who? The dog and the woman.

Their loyalty terrifies him. She offers to show him out the back door so he can get rid of them once and for all.

Quickly, he gets dressed and lets her lead him through a long, narrow hall, then down a staircase to the basement and out through a dark shaft leading to a back yard. Here she points towards a wall he'll have to climb over. It is reasonably tall and he hasn't climbed walls since he was a boy. So it's not strange that he feels great joy as he climbs over it.

As soon as he's over on the other side he begins to run, not worrying about the direction he's going in.

Outside the city it is as dusty as it is among the houses but the dust smells different. A strange sense of unity between himself and the countryside overcomes him and it keeps growing in this huge, calming emptiness.

He takes a deep breath, bends down to touch the sun-dried grass, gets back up and discovers a little clear-eyed, curious kid.

It seems natural that he would meet this boy right now. Without need to talk they decide to walk together.

They walk together for three or four kilometres. Then the boy turns around and runs so fast that in no time he turns into a distant dust cloud.

That such an important meeting should end in the fleeting dust seems unjust and without meaning to him. Despondent he plunks himself down in the flowers in the ditch and feels most of all like crying. Only when a dragonfly lands on his nose, positioned as if riding on the ridge of his nose, is he able to laugh again.

The next few kilometres he walks in bare feet. His shoes and socks he leaves behind in the ditch and soon he discovers just how sensitive the soles of his feet are. Without difficulty, and without having to look down, he avoids stepping on sharp stones.

The fields are more intensely green than any shade of green he's ever seen before, and the sky is more blue than any shade of blue he's ever seen. It isn't true that he likes grey cement more than green grass. This realization makes him so happy that for a moment he believes that he's reached the destination he thought he didn't know. However, when he reaches a set of railway tracks cutting right across everything doubt sets in as a red warning light stops him and a loud monotonous voice keeps repeating: DO NOT CROSS THE TRACKS —DO NOT CROSS THE TRACKS.

He begins to pick flowers on his side of the tracks. Carefully he selects each flower and arranges them delicately according to colour and size. Meanwhile a train roars past. Afterward, the silence feels complete.

As in a mirage he sees the building hover above the ground far away. It looks like the one he left which is why it seems at once appealing and threatening.

He feels sorry now that he left his socks and shoes behind in the ditch because the closer he gets to the building the harder the ground becomes. He winces and he starts to walk with a growing limp. He loses his concentration and so he doesn't manage to count the floors of the house as he steers directly toward the front door which proves to be locked. Though the front door of his own apartment building usually is locked, he feels snubbed here, perhaps because he doesn't recognize a single one of the names on the small labels beside each buzzer. He feels perplexed and discouraged and increasingly insecure as the sensation grows that he's being watched from everywhere. He grabs the door handle so hard that his knuckles turn white. Then he forces his shoulder up against the door and pushes with all his might. He has to get in to deliver the bouquet before it wilts, but time passes and the flowers already look limp and withered. Clouds drift across the bright summer sky making shadows on his back looking like x-ray pictures of dirty lungs. Some of the corolla from his bouquet sprinkle down on the sidewalk without him noticing.

Only when a family—father, mother, two small sons— returns from a picnic is he able to get into the building.

For a moment they try to prevent him but he slips by them and reaches the elevator before they do.

Frantically, he pushes one of the buttons realizing too late that it's the one for the basement. A few seconds later he finds himself in a dark hallway where he can just catch a glimpse of a row of padlocks and a row of doors. When his eyes have adjusted to the dark he discovers one of those light switches which leaves the light on for a few minutes before turning it off again. While the light is on he sees a rat disappear down a hole. He pushes the button for the elevator and goes up to the second floor.

The staircase he walks out onto is empty and without a sound, but light streams through a huge window through which he can see a similar staircase in the house next door. Over there a woman is in the process of working her way up the stairs with great effort. Between each landing she has to sit down and take a rest. When she sits down she looks like nothing more than an amorphous bundle kept together by a huge cobalt blue shawl. Life stirs in the bundle as she feels herself observed. She begins to wave but her movements are so heavy and tired she looks like she is expending her very last energy doing it.

He feels that he should help, not least because it won't cost him much with the windows separating them. Gesticulating he shows her the elevator. He wants her to understand that she doesn't have to exert herself with every step she takes. She shakes her head. She doesn't want to be enclosed which she shows him by holding on to her throat as if she were being strangled.

To show her that the elevator is safe he begins to drive up and down between the second and third floors. After each trip he gets out to look for her. She's not there and he is losing interest, when he suddenly notices her up on the third floor where she is tying her shoelace.

He considers it hopeless now to help her and he takes the elevator straight to the sixth floor, which must be right in the centre of the building because there are eleven buttons to choose from in addition to the one for the basement and the one marked HELP.

He chooses the door on the right and rings the doorbell. It opens so quickly one could get the impression that he was expected. He holds out his bouquet. Only the stems are left. The first bloom fell off while he was waiting to get into the building, the rest sprinkled down onto the basement floor, down on the elevator floor and on the stairs.

Before him stands a young man dressed in a purple silk suit. His hair is pitch black and it is slicked tightly to his head like a helmet. His eyelids are smothered with make-up in the same colour as his clothes and his long eyelashes are clumped into thick ropes with mascara. His lips, on the other hand, gleam colourlessly.

Shortly they are in the living room. Because of the heat the balcony door is open. On the balcony stands a woman with her back turned to the apartment, looking at the view. A thick fur coat hangs across the balcony rail which the woman leans against. She is naked. Her back and her rear end are white as mother of pearl.

Though she couldn't possibly avoid hearing the man dressed in purple saying thank you for the flowers she doesn't turn around. Now, he realizes that the man who's putting the flower stems into a vase might be a woman. His/her hands are incredibly small and smooth like silk and he thinks he's able to detect a light tremble from a pair of small breasts under his/her jacket.

He introduces himself to ascertain the truth but his own name is the only one mentioned.

The woman on the balcony stays as still as a statue. He goes out there and puts a hand on her behind which is cold as marble. She turns part way around towards him and smiles as if they were old acquaintances. Then, humming, she wraps herself in the fur coat and walks into the living room where she discovers the bouquet. Pulling it out of the vase and throwing it over the balcony she remarks that it seems more rare than it is beautiful. Then she calms down and sits down in the lap of the purple one. They begin to neck in such an uninhibited manner that he feels compelled to pace restlessly in the hope that they'll soon have had enough. But, whenever he passes in front of them he notices that their necking has increased.

The woman from the balcony has let her fur coat slide onto the floor and when the other one begins to slip out of his/her clothes he proves to be a man after all.

As their sighs and screams increase and their arms and legs get intertwined he begins to give up on getting into a conversation with them.

How they react to his slamming the front door behind him he will never know.

For a moment he considers whether he should try the apartment on the left but he decides to forget about it, deciding that it is probably right here in the middle of the building that necking flourishes. He therefore goes to the elevator but he doesn't know whether he wants to go up or down so he gets out of it again while he decides.

Leaning against the large window he falls into a deep meditation and he doesn't wake up until he recognizes the woman who earlier on was climbing the stairs between the second and third floors with such effort. Almost collapsed she strains to catch his attention but with un-ambiguous gestures he lets her know that he has important things to do.

In a state of panic she presses against the window and hammers on it with her fists. Naturally, he can't hear her but he can see her and he connects the image with his memory of the knocking on his front door and abruptly he takes the elevator to the ninth floor.

From here there's an incredibly gorgeous view. He can even see the building he used to live in until the moment he left it by going down the back stairs. He can also see the old part of town which looks like a collection of multicoloured building blocks from here. The park looks like a small green dot. Around this is the new, dull, section of town which will never get to look like toys no matter how far the distance becomes. It just looks like a bunch of identical paper boxes. Next to the conformity of the new section he sees the green fields which made him think that he had reached his destination. Ridiculous. After all, from this height one can clearly see that the railroad continues on from there. Like a worm it creeps out into the horizon and further still, but he let himself get stopped like a chicken reaching a drawn line. DO NOT CROSS THE TRACKS, and he didn't. Not even when the train had passed. He'd picked a bouquet of flowers which he'd now delivered to the wrong place.

In the neighbouring house the cobalt blue woman has reached the ninth floor and again she stands hammering shamelessly on the window to get his attention.

She can't possibly have got all the way up there walking step by step. She must have cheated. She must have taken the elevator despite the fact that she insisted that she was afraid. She has lied inexcusably. He detests her and in gestures he communicates to her just how deeply he loathes her. She doesn't seem to understand.

He gives up and takes the elevator all the way up to the eleventh and final floor where a big surprise awaits him.

Through a fireproof door he walks out on a patio on the roof with deck chairs and parasols. Apparently most of the tenants are sitting up here. They sit with drinks, magazines, newspapers and books. The sun is beating down so all the chairs are placed under the parasols, but even in the shadow the heat is so overwhelming that nobody is able to concentrate on their magazines, newspapers or books. The drink glasses, small and large, were emptied a long time ago. Nobody has the strength to turn their head or open their eyes as they hear him arrive.

Naturally, this disappoints him as his need to talk to somebody has increased by each passing floor. Now he has to depend on his faith that the view will redeem him and he walks toward the edge of the patio with anticipation.

There's an iron railing which has been extended up so high with wire netting that neither children nor adults would be able to push over it.

He looks out through the netting and since he has already established how far one can see from this building he chooses to look down in order to get the sensation of being up high.

Far, far down on the street a group of people have gathered around a bundle of clothes. It makes a very colourful picture composed of the multicoloured summer clothes worn by the gathering people and the cobalt blue bundle from which trickles a narrow line of red blood. It appears to be a frozen image which is only brought into movement when blinking blue lights get so close to the people that they seem to scatter like the debris from an explosion. A dog keeps circling the bundle but it is pushed away as they lift up the bundle and carry it away. None of the noise reaches him.

The silent movie he is watching here must be the end of a story he doesn't know and, as if in a effort to discover its beginning he lets his glance move up the neighbouring house, floor by floor, until he is looking at a roof patio like the one he himself is standing on. There he notices a hole in the wire netting which must have been cut with a pair of nippers or a heavy pair of scissors because it's impossible to tear this netting with bare hands.

Not only did she cheat and deceive him by taking the elevator first to the ninth floor and then to the eleventh, but it seems that she even carried a pair of nippers or a pair of scissors in her pocket because she knew all along what she wanted to do. Her pleading gestures were nothing but a big lie. A big imposition, which he, thank God, didn't fall for.

Laughing, he turns to the dozing people and encourages them to continue their apathy. He no longer has any need of them, he's not as easily fooled as they might think.

Despite his encouragements to the opposite everyone opens their eyes simultaneously and hones in on him like a group of searchlights. He runs out to the elevator and waits impatiently. It starts moving the first time he presses the button but it goes everywhere else but to the eleventh floor. He follows its movement as the numbered buttons light up. Now it's on the fifth floor, then it's on the eighth, then it ducks down into the basement. He presses hard on the button and stays there until the elevator comes all the way up without interruption.

He gets in. It seems to him that the most obvious button to push would be the one marked HELP. Not to call for help for himself, of course, but for the people on the patio who stayed in their deck chairs when the clothes bundle plunged down from the eleventh floor of the neighbouring house and lay bleeding on the street.

Didn't those people realize that the woman was screaming to be cared for, screaming for love? Of course, they knew, but they stayed in their chairs nonetheless, as if nothing had happened.

How could he make them comprehend how inexcusably they'd failed? By pushing the button marked HELP? If he pushes it will a man carrying a toolbox arrive and ask if the elevator is stuck? No, it's been driving for hours, he'll have to respond. "What's wrong then?", the repairman will ask impatiently. Since what is wrong cannot be fixed with tools, that's clearly not the button to push even though it seems so tempting his fingertip stays poised in front of it. However, now he forces the finger searchingly down over the entire panel of buttons.

Before he manages to decide someone else has chosen for him. The elevator has started and it stops on the third floor where a stranger opens the door. He runs the last stairs down to the ground floor where he exits.

A storm has come up. A piece of paper whirls toward him on the sidewalk, and the hair of the pedestrians flies about their heads. He enjoys the fact that he recently had his hair cut very short. Each hair on his head is only a couple of centimetres long. Effortlessly he gets on his way. Consciously he avoids checking to see if the wind has already dried out the line of blood to the point where it's lost the deep red colour he found so beautiful.

A PLACE TO BE HUMAN

Bo Green Jensen

It was raining in New Orleans.

Nothing strange about that. It had rained in Chicago, Austin, Washington, Milwaukee. Apparently it had also rained in all the other cities Daniel and Elisabeth had stayed in during the past 24 months. Whenever they'd had nothing else to talk about they could always fill the silence with talk about the weather. That was what they'd done in all the cities they passed through and so they did in New Orleans. Maybe they were growing old. An amazing amount of their lives was spent talking about the weather which never seemed quite to want to cooperate with them.

The rest of the time they made love, ate, travelled, read, went to the movies. Things weren't as bad as all that.

But the rain in Louisiana was different. It was grey and warm and quite soft. It began in the late morning when the air could retain no more moisture and unless the sun as an exception grew so hot that clear blue skies could burn through the haze the showers would continue the rest of the day.

The rain didn't last long but one always walked about under the skies in a stooped position, involuntarily bending forward constantly aware of the massive ceiling of clouds which cluttered the firmament.

In the old French section melancholy waiters stood on fragile cast iron balconies and observed the cloud formations with the laconic expression of people in the know. They spoke a lot about the skies. In this respect, Daniel and Elisabeth had come to the right place. In this city the weather was important. People didn't speak of much else.

It was late June and the season for tornadoes and hurricanes. Despite this there was little wind with the rain. One found oneself almost wishing that something would become of all the severe weather warnings. One almost wished for the big empty skies from the northern states up by the Canadian border.

One almost wished for so many things. But, as with the rain, there was nothing strange about that.

In New Orleans the greenhouse effect wasn't a frightening concept with a good name. It was real, it described conditions here, conditions which were chronic.

They stayed at a hotel on Canal Street. One night Daniel forgot to turn on the air conditioner and by the next morning their clothes were water-stained.

The air was like a wet robe wrapped closely around one's skin. Here one sometimes longed for a real rainstorm, cats and dogs, which did exist and happened up north where they'd had their base camp the past couple of years.

Here you sometimes longed for real rain and you could start crying just thinking about Danish weather. They were getting close to that point but a morning like this wasn't meant for homesickness.

True, the clouds had begun breaking open a little bit here and there, but the coffee was strong and hot, the egg fried to perfection and the bread lay golden on the white plates which reflected the light from the tall open windows onto their faces, making them squint and smile.

Daniel looked at Elisabeth in wonder. Hunger was spreading out from his stomach and into his solar plexus and from there into the rest of his body as it transformed into good, clean, uncomplicated desire. It was one of the thousand moments in a day when he was overwhelmed with desire for her and he was awed by the power of his need to get inside her.

Nothing strange about that. Since he got off drugs he regularly suffered these violent attacks of reproductive urges. Especially when he looked at Elisabeth. Making love to her was always close and good. Deep kisses in the softest of mouths.

He wasn't surprised at his hunger. In a week they were going back home to Denmark. This surprised him. He tried to imagine it. He couldn't. Elisabeth laughed because he sat there, his attention slipping away, disappearing into images of all the places they'd visited.

There was nothing strange about the rain or his longing or his desire. It was all that stuff about Denmark that was strange.

They sat in a restaurant on the corner of Bienville and Royal. The old town was actually a strained attempt at a set decoration of overvalued eateries, practically identical gift shops and shamelessly commercial bars.

These bars served hurricanes and highballs day and night to overweight tourists who all dressed in white shorts from Guatemala, wore hats made from palm leaves pulled down over their eyes and a stunned grin on their faces which had turned lobster red from too much gumbo and jambalaya, too many hurricanes and highballs and too much heat day in and day out.

It was a bizarre mixture of Hamburg, Paris, and the amusement park at Dyrehavsbakken in Copenhagen. This was Vieux Carre in New Orleans, Louisiana.

Nonetheless, Daniel enjoyed walking around there. Bourbon Street was too much, but Jackson Square was green and friendly, and he liked the cacophony of classical jazz, Zydeco, the gabbing of the tourists and the barkers' remarkable offering of magical nights in the meat market.

It would probably be more fun if one actually partook in the pandemonium, drank the booze and paid to bite into brown, Hispanic nipples, but it was still fine to walk about in the district staying transparent like a spy.

In this respect Daniel was still strange. Everybody else wanted to participate in the dance. He liked staying aloof. His treatment hadn't changed that.

When the clouds broke over Jackson Square they sought shelter in a store on the corner of Decatur and Saint Ann.

The store was filled with Americana, with special emphasis on the heritage of the South. Incidentally, all the souvenirs were manufactured in Taiwan, including the scale models of Tara and Twelve Oaks from *Gone With the Wind*, the fiftieth anniversary of which was being celebrated according to all the very best rules about recycling ideas and observing profitable anniversaries the film industry could muster. In the U.S. most things were manufactured on a license somewhere in Asia. It was the same up north.

In the square, which could have looked quite picturesque if it wasn't for the desperate attempt to make it look like Montmartre in Paris, complete with dogs, charlatans and a raw hunger for dollars, a small army of artists feverishly scattered with their works piled onto small pushcarts. They swore in three different languages and looked as if the hard rain for once had come as a surprise.

Behind them down by Moon Walk, the French Market and the river you could see the top of the paddle steamer, the *Mississippi Queen*, and in the park the palm trees nourished themselves on the rain. The magnolia bloomed, poisonous and healthy. They were far away from the world of the pedestrian street in Copenhagen at Christmas time, but still there wasn't much separating a rainy day in New Orleans from being drenched during the Roskilde Music Festival. The wet colours looked alike.

Denmark suddenly appeared like that in the strangest places. There was no end to it and it was beginning to irritate them even if they were homesick. Their homesickness was not a real longing. It was rather a way of neutralizing their longing. The Denmark they thought about and talked about had nothing to do with the real Denmark which they knew, could remember and which they were constantly reminded of when a confluence of moods produced an accidental air of recognition.

Their time in exile affected them in this way. If they hadn't actually turned into Americans they were well on their way to becoming Rebild Danes. They nurtured a picture postcard image of Denmark, and sentimentality seemed to an increasing extent to be both real and essential, more important than many drives of a more healthy, bloody and constructive nature.

Not much new in that. Daniel had always been prone to nostalgia. Now he lived in the perfect circumstance for it. What was new was that Elisabeth felt the same way. Slowly they agreed that there really was only the weather left to talk about.

They turned their backs to the rain pouring down the windows and started in a determined manner to study the exclusive junk store's mixed inventory of rubbish, kitsch and good stuff. In this way Elisabeth got a complete set of figurines of all the characters from another golden anniversary movie, *The Wizard of Oz*.

Daniel concentrated on Civil War stuff. But he almost fell for the tin soldiers of the new era: all the characters from *Lord of the Rings* placed in a carved box. Just a handsome little item for close to a thousand dollars and *he* really felt tempted!

It was no use denying it. If you took the trouble you could sell almost anything to Daniel and Elisabeth.

They were just like all the other tourists. Though they weren't overweight and though they didn't drink hurricanes or highballs they still eagerly sought out all the shops in the area and Daniel, especially, was unable to remain unaffected by all the special offers. He was sober, abstinent and completely clean for his second year now. So, how else was he going to spend his time?

Consequently, they bought intricately decorated belt buckles with the Dixie symbol emblazoned in red, white and blue, "Louisiana" set in relief and screaming eagles placed symmetrically. They'd gathered a collection of lapel emblems, one for each state they'd visited. They invested in an expensive Batman mug, scale models of Tara, Twelve Oaks and more, an authentic Indiana Jones hat made by Stetson and very fashionable T-shirts with Hard Rock Cafe, New Orleans written on them.

Daniel enjoyed getting childish. He felt unrestrained and after two days he looked like all the other tourists in the city. He wore white shorts from Guatemala, a hat made from palm leaves pulled down over his eyes and often he caught himself smiling in the rain because actually he did feel good about the world, right here right now, the past year, the year to come, and Elisabeth who increasingly filled up his life.

Perhaps thirteen was his lucky number. They had been to thirteen states. They had been married for thirteen years. He was in love with his wife and he was as clean as he'd been at the dawning of the '60s.

He couldn't remember ever feeling this good. If he could only get a fix on all that stuff about Denmark there wouldn't be a cloud in his world.

By the way, Daniel was a writer by profession. He hadn't written a word in two years. "So what?" he said to himself whenever he was suddenly reminded of this tiny dark spot on the otherwise bright and colour-saturated screen of his life. "So what if I have nothing to write about? I've never felt better. We've never had it better. I'm rich. I'm full. There's nothing more I want to say. New Orleans is after all a place to be human. It's good to stay over for a week here."

And he said this so often that he finally believed it. They'd arrived Wednesday. They'd flown from Minneapolis to Houston early in the morning, changed planes and finally landed in Louisiana at the end of a long afternoon.

Everybody in Minnesota had told them, "If you think this is hot just wait till you get to New Orleans."

Daniel and Elisabeth had thought that no matter what, things could hardly get worse or hotter than they were in Minneapolis. After a long Winter with snow and temperatures of -30° it had turned into a horrible Spring with 30 degree heat every day in a matter of two weeks. That is, 100 degrees Fahrenheit as they said over here.

The American system was harder to calculate but it gave a better impression of the intensity of the heat, for example.

It really did feel like it was 100 degrees.

It's true that New Orleans was worse. Here you stepped out into a sauna of misty rain and you were constantly blinded by the light from the dull, chronically hazy sky. However, this kind of sky fit the place with its disintegrating humidity, its accent on extreme motion. You'd really reached the outer edge of the land of the latest stuff. They were further away from home than ever before. Even the Mississippi disappeared down here.

The first day they were tired. They got booked into Canal Street, found their bearing in the French Quarter where they were seduced into eating cajun fish for $100 in a slightly too exclusive restaurant on Bourbon Street, found their way down to Jackson Square and the river, and walked home to their room.

The next day they spent on a day trip through the Garden District where the old houses were stunningly huge and often in hues of blue and pink, standing under dense and lush greens. They walked through the old English quarter which was as empty as a ghost town.

At one of the incredible graveyards—called Cities of the Dead—a Cuban police officer insisted on taking them safely through the black neighbourhoods. His offer annoyed them. They hadn't asked for special treatment. They were used to walking in the black neighbourhoods. They had never run into trouble, but that's what it meant being from Denmark: You were always treated as particularly fragile guests. Again, he was reminded of Denmark and all that. It was impossible to get away from it.

They drove down the Esplanade out to the park district and even though it rained as usual they began to understand the joy people here felt at living in New Orleans.

In Canal Street it was hard to find the reason for that joy. Here there was garbage, neon lights and blacks waiting around who either ignored them or smiled at Eli. Presumably they were waiting around for transportation. It was difficult to tell. There was always a group standing at the corner of Rampart and Canal.

It could easily have been the same people waiting around all the time.

Time passed and the days began melting together. They drove into the swamplands and they looked at old French plantations. The *Cajun Queen* took them down the river to Chalmette where park police in historical uniforms reconstructed the Battle of New Orleans. One tired from listening to their hoarse screams though their intention was good enough. Their minds began to float on the wind out here in the open country where a yellow sandstone house stood alone flanked by the flat grey marsh and trees with large crowns.

There were lots of turtles and pelicans out here but they never caught sight of an alligator. On the other hand, the local red necks had filled up the bayou canals along Huey Long Drive with empty beer cans, used condoms and read or unread copies of the local daily, *The Picayeune*.

They did their best to disappear without a trace in Louisiana. They had succeeded in Minnesota. The problem was that up there you were almost constantly reminded that a place called Denmark existed. Most of the Midwest had begun somewhere in Scandinavia.

It was better in New Orleans. Only a very few people knew

of those countries here. One impression killed the next. Memories of various situations began overlapping, erasing each other and mixing together in an uncertain noise. In the midst of all this Daniel held onto his constant vision of Elisabeth. Among these white houses he thought in the darkness of his heart that it would be possible to forget one's name here. Here, a soul could leave on the wind.

This condition was quite pleasant. You didn't constantly think of Denmark.

At the hotel he read *Lucky-Per*. It was one way to return home, he thought, or at least to prepare for landing at Kastrup Airport which would happen in four days no matter whether they'd got used to the idea or not.

Up north in three different houses in the twin cities of Minneapolis and St. Paul, where Daniel had been Visiting Professor in Scandinavian literature, they had spent three semesters nursing their homesickness. Daniel wrote in Danish whenever he could and Elisabeth sent home an endless stream of letters.

Everything around them took place in English and they were good at English, the language wasn't the problem, but still they caught themselves longing for home. It was a completely absurd longing. They were both aware of that. But that didn't decrease it.

They couldn't escape the fact that they were Danish. If it were possible they'd have done so a long time ago.

Up in Wisconsin back in the deep winter when everything was at its whitest he had been sitting reading *Jørgen Stein* while their American friends who were along on the ski trip spent the evening singing worn-out folk songs, wiping dried pieces of food off the faces of their kids and holding championships in such apparently global games as Cheat, Monopoly and Chinese Checkers.

In Texas he had given guest lectures on *Niels Lyhne* and on Ole Jastrau. In his hotel room in Washington he'd read *The Liar*. It had felt like a meaningful project to finish off by getting to know the fictitious Sidenius more inti-mately and the first volume of *Lucky-Per* had formed the perfect companion piece to Spring burning its way through the earth in Minnesota.

In various motels in North Dakota, in towns like Moorhead, Bismarck, Mandan and Lakota—towns he'd never heard of or ever dreamt he would hear of—he had travelled through most of the second volume and he'd not encountered any difficulties in keeping the two worlds apart. George Armstrong, Custer and Sitting Bull. Per Sedenius and Doctor Nathan. The road to Kærsholm and Inger in Denmark. The road to Little Big Horn and Mon-tana.

No problem at all.

However, down in New Orleans, in the hotel with the blue swimming pool and the jacuzzi, Daniel had reached the end of his journey. In the novel Per Sidenius explored as far into the unknown of Jutland as possible. Daniel both understood him and didn't. He himself was sitting at the furthest edge, as far down south as it's possible to get in North America, and the feeling of evaporation which suf-fused everything blurred the border between *Lucky-Per* and Louisiana. Daniel was unable to hold on to anything any longer, neither the reality of New Orleans nor the re-ality of Pontoppidan's novel. He thought that he ought to shut the book and forget about it, forget about leaving and stay in Louisiana, the state where the Mississippi disappears.

It was not the first time he'd had thoughts like that. At the geographical centre of the continent, in Rugby, North Dakota, way up by the border to Manitoba, Canada, he had thought the very same thought and felt the same way.

He had heard a voice say, "Then go and stay in Memphis," and it had both irritated and saddened him that no feeling at all seemed to be devoid of some literary resonance and be without some anchoring in tradition.

At one point during the first couple of months in Minneapolis when everything was new, foreign and actually not at all inviting, their house, the teaching, the new quiet in their lives which wasn't able to drown out the screeching cars on Lyndale Avenue, he had quoted to himself out loud the words from *The Fall of the King* almost as a challenge:

"I lost the true Spring of my life in Denmark longing for happiness in foreign lands. But on my travels I did not find that happiness, for everywhere I longed for my native hearth. And when all the world finally could tempt me no more then Denmark too had died in my heart and I became homeless."

Daniel still wasn't certain that he understood the very depth of this quote. Also, he wasn't quite sure that he *wanted* to understand it, but he felt certain of this: that he would not stay in Memphis, he would not stay in Minneapolis and he did not want to die alone in a New Orleans deserted even by the sphinx.

He wanted to go back to Denmark together with Elisabeth and they were leaving on Tuesday.

On the balcony eight floors above the street, where the blue swimming pool was gleaming and shimmering as the sun danced over it producing the illusion of wind, and air you could breathe, Elisabeth was engaged in a conversation with a black couple from Alabama.

They were holidaying with their children. Daniel didn't get involved in the conversation which essentially consisted of Elisabeth for the thousand and first time explaining to strangers what Denmark was, where it was, how the weather there was, who they were and all that, while he himself looked up from his book and contentedly began to covet his neighbour's wife.

She was a heavy woman, perfect in her own way, buxom and dark like the exquisitely-shaped magnolia he had seen in the marshes at Chalmette. Her body glistened in the sun. Her movements filled the air with electric charges which made the moment vibrate. She giggled and chirped uncertainly, not used to being so helpless and exposed in an open pool of cool water.

A little later she sought refuge in the warm jacuzzi. Through the shimmering heat you could glimpse the traces of her movements. The children followed her through the magnetic field. You could forget your sense of hunger for a woman like that. You could forget your name and your world, your country.

Daniel and her husband exchanged glances, looked at the women and shared a smile which was without place and time. Daniel wasn't jealous of the man who had forgotten his hunger because of this woman, but if he'd had to make the choice between being a family man from Alabama and the Daniel who'd burned himself up in Denmark, as he remembered it, he would without hesitation have chosen to be the black man.

The treatment had changed all that and there would be no choice to make. He could stay here, in a state of fulfilled longing, in the sun in New Orleans, eight floors above street level, where the voices of the children became swallows in the air, where his homesickness and all his half memories turned into dust because all that was left here was desire, desire to stay in the sun, to become one with the sun.

Daniel looked at Elisabeth. In his solar plexus his hunger began to work and with each heartbeat Denmark died a little more. Elisabeth smiled. The water sprang off her body like sparks. For her he wanted to forget his name and his world.

He closed *Lucky-Per* and put away the book. There was no reason to finish it. In a sun chair across from him a German woman lay reading Maurice Denuzier's *Louisiana*, a huge colourful legend with lots of material to forget and to believe in.

"Yes", thought Daniel. "Yes, dammit! That's exactly the kind of book to sit and read here!"

On the last day Daniel was strong. There was nothing else for him to work out about Denmark. There was nothing else for him work out about the U.S. And there was nothing else he needed to write. From now on he would speak up. He had lost the true Spring of his life and he'd become homeless long ago but he did find his happiness in a foreign land. It lived in Elisabeth's eyes. It lived between Elisabeth's thighs.

On the Tuesday the Danish couple left for home. Where they are now no one knows for certain but I wonder if they might not sit somewhere in the sun longing for New Orleans?

Elisabeth is explaining to their guests what Minnesota is, where it is, how the weather is there, who they themselves are and all that.

Daniel sits by himself reading. He's wearing white shorts from Guatemala. His hat made from palm leaves is pulled down over his eyes. The book he's reading looks like *Louisiana* by Maurice Denuziere. If it isn't *North and South* by John Jakes. Or even, the sacred *Gone With the Wind*.

But there is no doubt about the fact that the Danish kids are back home.

ONE OF THE LITTLE SAVIOURS

Ulla Ryum

Simultaneously, they both felt that the time had come.

One of them was surrounded by her husband, two midwives and a professor of births.

The other was on her way down from the summer pastures, walking among the sheep.

The first one heard the rain begin outside. A young midwife closed the window right away.

The second one tied her skirt around her waist, took off her shoes and her socks and put them in her backpack. Then she opened a huge umbrella and tried to peer out through the rain.

The first one's husband held her hand and the professor asked about the well-being of mutual friends. Her husband answered. She heard the rain faintly on the window. She smiled at the men and prepared herself for a new contraction.

The second one could see through the gusts of wind that the large flock of sheep had gathered behind the rocks a little above her and between contractions she crawled up to them. They had turned their backs to the wind and she forced her way into the middle of the group. The storm increased and she pulled down her umbrella as far as she could without hurting the sheep closest to her.

The first one was given a mask through which she could receive laughing gas. She didn't want it. The midwife who was standing between her out-spread legs asked her to breathe as she had been instructed earlier. She did and her husband checked his watch. She knew that he was going to perform tonight. They had agreed that he shouldn't cancel. This was their second child. She thought about her five-year-old son. She wondered if her parents could get him to sleep. He was going through a phase where he refused to sleep at night. She hoped that he would like the new baby. She inhaled deeply just as the midwife had instructed her, then quickly and shallowly. She followed all the instructions coming from the happy face between her knees. She felt like laughing as she let herself get caught by the oncoming contraction. She turned her head toward the window and she felt the rain fill her body. She was giving birth to the earth.

The second one used her freed hand to feel the earth between her legs and then she raked together as much grass as she could without letting go of the umbrella. The sheep squeezed her and she just managed to bless them before she grabbed hold of the wool of the nearest sheep as the next contraction came on. The sheep stood petrified as the storm howled past their bowed heads. She couldn't hear the thunder any longer. She hoped her other children had found shelter. But they were not familiar with the weather this time of year. She didn't have the strength to concentrate on anything other than holding on to the umbrella. She could feel with her free hand that the baby's head was on its way.

Like a warm stream water was running down over her fingers and legs. It wasn't rain water. She cried. A strange heavy sense of sorrow was at work in her body. She had known for days that her baby wouldn't live. Its movements had been hesitant, unwilling.

She'd known because in her dreams she'd heard the baby call in the opposite direction. Away from her.

The other seven children she had given birth to had all called toward her. She'd been able to answer them. She'd been able to sing to them and call them into the light when their time had arrived.

This child wanted to leave even before it was born.

She knew that it'd rather live among the other unborn, dead children. All the little saviours whose bright faces lit up to help those who sought help in the night.

She managed to tie the umbrella onto one of the

straps on her back pack. As she supported herself on two sheep she felt the baby's head working its way through.

The first one was called back from a long undulating contraction by the voice of the professor who asked her to work and not to rest. The midwives were busy between her legs. Her husband whispered encouragingly, asking her if she wanted the mask. She didn't. A sudden anger grabbed hold of her. She heard herself swear in a loud, strange voice. She sensed their surprise at her sudden violent reaction. Then the professor put a calming hand on her husband's arm and whispered something to him after which they both looked understandingly at her.

She felt betrayed by all of them.

Why the hell were they meddling? She was doing what she was supposed to. She wanted to get up and tell them to go to hell with their nonsense and instructions but she only got halfway there when she met the eyes of one of the midwives, the older one, the one she'd been a little scared of all the time. She looked deep into the bottom of her eyes and suddenly she felt understood, accepted. She heard the midwife tell the rest of the group that she and the midwives could handle things from here. Her husband kissed her goodbye and wished her a good day's work. The two men laughed. Good feelings had been re-established. She didn't care. He called to her that he'd be in touch after the first act. The professor also left, smiling at her husband's stupid joke. Finally there was quiet.

The old midwife opened the window and the fresh, humid air dense with rain hit her with an indescribable sense of happiness. She noticed the young midwife standing for a moment at the open window. Then the young midwife sat down to work at the desk beneath the window.

She knew it was now. The rain streamed down over her, in her. She was giving birth to the earth—it would slide down over the mountain like a spruce cone on a foaming river of rain water. She pushed and inhaled. She drifted away again, passing over the bowed head of the young midwife and let herself float along with the clouds. Beneath her she noticed a large flock of sheep slowly moving down over the mountain. She immediately recognized the spot. They had stayed there for three days during their holidays last year. She could see the place between the white rocks where they had made love and she became pregnant.

She heard herself moan in pleasure. Then she saw the old midwife's face speaking to the young one who got up and came over.

One more time, the old one said, and the young one dried her face with a cold cloth. She closed her eyes in an attempt to hold on to the vision of the flock of sheep below her but she had to shift her concentration to a violent contraction. She pushed and thought of the thousands of paths the sheep had carved into the mountain. She could sense the scent of rocks warmed by the sun and of herbs. Suddenly she was thrown out into a violent circling movement and she grabbed in the air as if trying to fly. The young midwife held on to her. She noticed that she was almost standing up in the bed. Then she slumped back, exhausted and overwhelmed as she felt her tears running down her cheeks.

She heard her baby scream.

The other one could feel the little body fall out. She softened the fall as well as she could with one hand. She let herself sink down against the wet, soft sides of the sheep to rest for a moment—a couple of minutes maybe—maybe longer.

She was outside time.

The rain was no longer as heavy and she could hear the cicadas and the bells on the sheep. They'd slowly begun grazing again.

She leaned forward and sought out the little cold body in the grass between her legs. She could tell that the child was dead but she lifted it up and kissed it. He was a boy.

She bit off the umbilical cord and found a kerchief in

her pack. She wrapped the little bluish baby in it. Then she sat on her haunches and pushed out the placenta. She was exhausted and rested curled up against her back pack. The sheep she had held on to while giving birth to the dead child still stood by her side as if they knew that she needed them. The rest of the flock had spread out over the mountainside and she could hear their bells and the barking of the two dogs.

She noticed that she bled every time she moved so she lay back down again. She shut her eyes and dozed off.

The air was filled with insects again and the warm air did her good. The rocks near her steamed in the sun and the two sheep pushed her with their heads. She succeeded in folding the umbrella back again. She was found several hours later by her husband and a couple of other shepherds with the umbrella at her side and the little dead boy in her arm.

A big girl, the first one heard the midwives say together.

She looked in curious wonder at the little red, wrinkled and greasy body lying on her stomach. The young midwife was putting a label around the baby's wrists. It's the number and time of birth, the old midwife said as if responding to the question in her mind. They are easily mistaken for one another. The young midwife took the baby again and the old one prepared for the last part of the job. While she listened to her daughter scream loudly and continuously, clearing herself out to be ready for life, the old midwife pushed out what was left of her internal secrets. Finally she received her husband's accolades over the telephone. The first act had gone well and now everyone had gathered around him, congratulating him and sharing a bottle in celebration of his daughter.

The professor arrived with a bottle of wine and everyone was happy. The baby was asleep and she noticed that she had her father's nice little ears. That made her happy. Suddenly and violently she longed to see the grazing flock of sheep again. She hoped it hadn't disappeared. Far away she heard the sound of it. She closed her eyes and fell into a sleep of exhaustion.

The other one woke up when they lifted her off the ground.

With some difficulty she was able to stand up. The sleep had done her good and she wasn't bleeding so much any longer. Her husband brought the little dead boy in her kerchief. One of the sheep dogs had apparently eaten the placenta. The two other men took off their hats and she nodded to them. She still felt distant in time and consciousness.

It was a boy, wasn't it? her husband asked quietly. She nodded again and for a moment she felt overwhelmed by the unearthly sorrow she'd experienced earlier.

He was one of the little saviours, she heard him say quietly to the two other men. One by one all three of them took her hands and kissed them awkwardly.

First her husband, then the two others.

Then her husband picked up his gun and called the dog who'd eaten the placenta. She felt dizzy, sat down on a rock and looked away. The dog came slowly towards her husband. She wanted to stop him. The shot rang out.

The dog made a half-turn in the air, fell down and lay quietly, stretched out. She looked at her husband then at the ground. She heard him whisper that it'd been a good dog.

He had to do it because it had tasted his blood, she thought, and she got up with an effort. She wanted to get away from this spot. Home. It had to be.

The men had gathered the flock and started to move down the mountain.

She was tired, exhausted, but no longer did she feel outside of time and deplete of life.

She carried her sorrow.

Her husband carried the little dead saviour.

On the morning of the fifth day the husband of the

first one came to bring her and the newborn daughter home. In the car downstairs their five-year-old son waited in anticipation to see his new little sister.

He'd been very disappointed to learn that he wasn't allowed on the ward. He'd rather have chosen his sister himself from among all the new kids his father had told him about. Besides he'd rather have had a little brother.

Finally they showed up and a moment later his little sister was right next to him on the back seat. His mother showed him her little sleeping face half hidden in the blankets in the cot. He thought she was way too small and he wasn't allowed to hold her till they got home. Her mother got in next to his father in the front seat and they drove off through town.

His mother turned around to see if the cot was safe. He didn't want to look after his sister like his dad asked him to. He wanted to go to his mother and sit on her lap like he used to.

He was almost all the way over onto the front seat, despite the fact that his father had tried to force him back with his arm, when the accident happened.

In the quiet after the crash the cry of the newborn baby was heard in the wrecked car.

She was the only survivor.

THE LADY

Niels Hav

The morning is raw. He leaves his apartment around nine. He doesn't have to go anywhere in particular. He finds his rhythm automatically, his feet are used to walking. His steps traverse the concrete sidewalk as he passes parked wrecks and street corners. He doesn't have to keep an eye on the little green man. The sound of the traffic rises and falls with the accompanying exhaust. That's sufficient for him.

He usually walks in this direction but the actual streets he takes may vary. You could imagine that the houses recognize him, but they don't. They are dreaming. He wants to get through the city and then return. In reality he is transparent. He's well aware of that. He's nothing but a pair of eyes.

So what!

He passes a place where the pigeons are hovering over the sidewalk hacking at each other. The man in the hot dog stand laughs and serves someone a regular hot dog with remoulade sauce and ketchup.

"Damned pigeons," he says.

An enormous parka manoeuvres the hot dog which disappears into the hood in short jerky movements. He sits down on the bench and lets his eyes move about, gawking. The parka swallows the bun, but one piece won't go down. He crumbles the piece of bread between his fingers and hurls it at the pigeons.

"Damned pigeons," the hot dog vendor says and opens a cola. "They are useless. Aren't they?"

He feels his ass getting wet. There's water on the bench. He gets up and continues on his way. He might well have been able to eat a hot dog, or a pigeon, but he only has half a fistful of coins in his pocket and he wants to spend them indoors.

The sun can be seen glistening between two gables. He walks on. The cheese shop, the green grocer's, the butcher, the book worm, the jewellery pig, the super mammal. A red-headed girl passes him. She, too, looks straight through him.

Well? Onwards.

Butcher, coffee lady, clothing man, hardware guy, cheese man, money tank, clothing lady. His feet know every flagstone. Pretty well.

At the roundabout he stops to buy smokes. He sits down and watches the carrousel. Cars in all colours whirl around, signalling, making noise and smelling. His eyes grow into a fixed position, an hour disappears like a forgotten smoke left between two fingers.

His stomach growls. He gets up and begins to walk back downtown. He passes everything in reverse. He is an awake sleepwalker. He lets his feet guide him. Cement, glass, steel. What's a body to do against that?

Music.

He walks through the automatic doors and goes straight up to the music section. He asks to hear Devo. The clerk hesitates, he needs to have it spelled out. DEVO.

He stands listening to the music.

Afterwards he jumps on the escalator and is taken up through the various departments. Clothes and shoes are cued up waiting to be served. On the top floor he walks into the cafeteria and picks up a tray. He looks over the menu and chooses a well-topped sandwich and takes a cola. He pays and waits for an empty table.

While he's eating he doesn't see anything. He tastes his food and feels it in his stomach. Only afterwards does he notice the other tables. They are all occupied by people in proper attire. He burps and pulls out his smokes. He is not invisible in here. Some of the people sitting closest to him look at him with their polite eyes.

Then the lady appears. She stops and looks around.

There are no empty tables.

"Is this taken?" She smiles sweetly.

He shakes his head.

She eases her tray down on the table, hangs her purse over the chair and strips off her coat.

"It's warm in here."

"Yes, it is." He coughs and moves his cola to give her more room. She looks fit and is well made up, pretty to look at.

"I'm exhausted... All those people."

He tries to smile. His face feels tight. On her tray are a salad, a tiny loaf of bread and cup of coffee. She sits down and nibbles at her salad.

"We're also here," he says.

"Well, yes." She eats. Her lips receive the fork in a motherly fashion and encloses the salad. The jaws start their work. She breaks off a small piece of bread and pops it in.

He smokes and lets his eyes wander.

"I like your hair," she says, "how does it feel?"

"Feel?" His fingers go through his hair. What a bitch, he thinks.

"May I try?" Her hand is already cruising through his hair.

"Don't!" he says overwhelmed and moves his head away. He almost lost his cigarette.

"Oh, come on," she says, "you're not made out of glass, are you?"

The people at the neighbouring table leave. Three men and a woman push their chairs back in and walk towards the exit with secure, calm movements. They barely make eye contact with their surroundings. Perhaps they are on their way back to an office where important matters await their decisions.

She pushes her plate to the middle of the table and puts the purse in her lap. Her hands are well-kept, but slightly agitated. They find her cigarette case and pull out a Prince.

"D'you have a light?"

He lights his lighter and reaches it across the table, keeping his arm stiff.

"I like it here," she says and looks around. "Whenever I have a day off, I come down here to shop. I usually time it so I can have lunch here." She looks directly at him and exhales smoke under the lamp. "The food here is so delicately prepared."

Delicate. He pulls at his chair and looks at her. Beneath the make-up there are tiny wrinkles under her eyes, but they are almost invisible.

"Don't you think so?"

"I don't know... It tastes good."

She smiles broadly. "It does, doesn't it? And the atmosphere, I like the pastels. They make the room feel spacious and they are so..." She raises a hand and looks for the word in the air. "...aesthetic."

"Shit," he says and squashes the butt of his cigarette in the ashtray.

"What do you mean?" Delighted, she giggles.

"Aesthetic!" he sneers.

She laughs and leans in over the table. Her breasts pitch under her sweater. "They are beautiful, don't you think? That's all I'm saying."

He pulls out a fresh cigarette from his jacket and lights it.

"Can I get you a cup of coffee?" she says and gets up holding a cup in each hand.

"Please," he says surprised.

She goes over to the counter. He follows her with his eyes. She pours the coffee and he studies her body. The outline of her rear end looks impressive under her skirt. Delicate and aesthetic, he thinks. Carefully she keeps her balance on her way back between the tables with a cup in each hand.

"Don't thank me," she says and puts the cup in front

of him. He tastes the coffee. It is acidic and muddy. But it's coffee nonetheless.

"Why are you sitting here?" she says. "Don't you have anything to do?"

"Nope." He hesitates for a moment. "We could go home to your place."

She laughs hysterically and looks around. A natural colour shows up under her make-up.

"No," she says, alarmed, "we can't do that."

"Why not?"

"We just can't. But I think you're cute." She reaches over to touch him. He holds on to her fingers with his teeth and touches their tips with his tongue. They taste salty, but there's another taste as well.

"I do like you," she says quickly. "It's too bad with all that unemployment. Young people graduate and they have nothing to do. When you meet them on the street they want to pass you quickly. They hide. The government really should do something, it's terrible. But often I think: why don't they do something themselves? There are so many possibilities, right?"

He lets go of her hand and she bends her fingers and studies her nails.

"What kinds of possibilities?" he says.

"Well, I don't know. Start something. Travel, for example. There's a whole wide world out there just waiting."

"Where the hell should we go? It's the same all over."

"I know. But still... you're young, right?"

People get up and leave. The lunch crowd is shrinking. A girl wearing a brown tunic pulls a cart between the tables and picks up plates and glasses. She works concentratedly, emptying the ashtrays and cleaning them quickly with a cloth.

"The world is a boil," he says.

She laughs. "Well, with that attitude you certainly

won't get far, I can tell you that."

"Get far?! You people don't understand a damned thing. Do you think we want to take over your stinking jobs which keep you tied to the same routine day in and day out? You drag yourselves around wearing blinkers."

"You're cute," she says smiling. "But what is it you want then?"

"Baah." He sits up in his chair and collects his things. "I don't want to talk to you anymore."

"Okay," she says and gets up. "I'd better get home in any case." She pulls on her coat. "It's good to have a home... You have a home, too, don't you?"

"Of course, I have a home," he says and thinks about his space, its slowly shifting light, his comics and the enervating dripping of the water faucet.

She smiles with satisfaction.

"That's good," she says. "Then try and be a little happier."

He looks at her. Her eyes are losing their power; they're becoming small and hard. She attempts to get the strap of her purse over one shoulder and to wave good-bye at the same time, but the move fails, and for a moment her face looks naked. She looks frightened.

Then she's on her way. The sound of her heels drowns in the noise between the tables. He follows her. On the way down the escalator he catches a glimpse of her neck which already looks as if it could belong to anybody.

He's back on the street. The light has changed and the traffic has grown more dense. His feet find their rhythm and he's in motion.

THE STAIN

Astrid Saalbach

She is standing in the blue semi-darkness of the wings watching the performance on stage. He walks back and forth, speaking. This is his big soliloquy. The audience is completely silent. They always are at this point.

His costume suits him. It emphasizes his body and makes him look even more masculine and sensual. Beate laughed when she told her that and reminded her that he was old enough to be her father and, besides, that he preferred his own sex.

His soliloquy is finished. Applause. The show continues.

Her cramps are getting heavier. Pain is shooting across her loins and she's sweating. She bends over and leans against a tree made from papier mâché decorated with light green paper leaves which will be used in the last scene when Spring has returned.

"Do you have cramps?" Beate, who's playing the maid, whispers.

Ida nods.

"Do you want a painkiller? I have some that usually work."

"No thanks. I've already taken two, I can't risk taking more."

"Poor girl."

Beate caresses her arm lightly.

Ida's cue is approaching. She lets go of the tree and enters.

Her concentration and the heat from the lights make the pain take on a different character. The shooting pain stops and instead a throbbing sensation settles into her bloated abdomen.

Her voice sounds different. Darker. Slightly

hoarse. As if it were someone else's. She walks over to the window and looks out on the naked, black trees. Discreetly, she tries to loosen her corset. It is so tight she can barely breathe.

Beate enters to announce that the carriage is ready.

He calls her over. One of the other actors accidentally steps on her dress. She trips and almost falls but he catches her, gives her a peck on each cheek and wishes her a pleasant journey.

She fumbles her way out through the curtains into the darkness. She is drenched with sweat. She leans against the tree. She doesn't have to go on again for some time. The young woman doesn't return from her trip until the very end of the play.

"Beate? Would you please open up my dress?"

"Don't breathe ... There we are! That better?"

"Yes, thank you."

She slips down on her haunches.

"You should lie down before you're on again."

"Where?"

"There's a divan in his dressing room. He's on stage most of the time anyway."

The stage manager shushes them.

"I'm embarrassed to ask..." she whispers.

"Then I'll ask for you."

She and Beate share a dressing room. It's a small, narrow room with just enough space for the table with two mirrors, a couple of chairs, a cupboard and a clothes rack for costumes. He has his own dressing room which is evidently large enough for a divan.

She slips casually into hiding between the curtains when he comes backstage a little later. Beate approaches him. He nods and smiles in a friendly manner. Then he begins to talk to the young man.

"It's fine. Go on up and lie down. I'll make sure that you get your call."

She limps out into the foyer, across the hall and up all the stairs to the dressing rooms. She stops in front of the large mirror. She's pale under her make-up and there are dark lines under her eyes. The pain makes her nauseous. This time is worse than usual. Perhaps because she's tired and tense. Even though she's only got a small part it's the largest one she's ever had.

His dressing room is at the end of the corridor. She opens the door and enters. The light is on and the curtains pulled shut. It is getting dark outside.

She takes off her dress and hangs it carefully across a chair so it won't be wrinkled. She keeps on her slip and her top.

What a relief to lie down. She lies completely still, her eyes closed. A subtle scent of perfume tickles at her nose. She opens her eyes. At the foot of the divan hangs a thick deep red velour dressing gown. For a moment she thinks it's moving, bending down over her. On the floor under the divan stands a pair of slippers made of the same fabric. She looks around the room without turning her head...

There's a table with a make-up kit carefully arranged according to kind and colour into separate compartments. Not like hers and Beate's which is in a mess of melted rouge, eye shadow, eye liner, broken lipsticks and mascara, all mixed up and sprinkled with a thin layer of powder. On the light blue towel next to the make-up lies a black moustache from another show. Above the table hangs a mirror and next to it a bulletin board with call sheets, letters of thanks, invitations to film openings and things of that nature, and a photo of a ballet dancer. Handsome and glistening with sweat. He looks at her with a little smile and peculiarly inscrutable eyes.

She curls up in pain and pulls up her legs. She shivers with cold. On a chair by the window lies a beige blanket. She can just reach it by crawling down to the foot of the divan. It is soft and light as a feather and it smells just like a dressing gown. She holds her stomach and rocks back and forth till she runs out of energy. Then she lies completely still. She feels good here. Protected. Fragile. Weak. Hidden. The distant sound of the trickle in the water pipes. The soft yellow of the walls. The pitching dressing gown raining its fragrance down over her. The quiet. The orderliness. She stretches and gives in to the pain. She lets it wash over her like a flood. She drowns herself in it. The pain feels sweet. The blood feels warm as it trickles distantly in the pipes. She feels blissful. She's floating ...

She is awakened by the knock on the door.

"Last scene coming up." It's the stage manager's voice.

"Thank you!"

She sits up slowly. The pain has disappeared. She gets up and puts on her shoes and her dress. She can't close it herself; she'll have to ask Beate or one of the others to help her. She looks in the mirror. Her eyes are clear and the dark lines have gone. All she has to do is put on a little powder before going back down.

Then she sees it. In the middle of the beige blanket there's a huge red blotch. She bled through while she slept.

She picks up the blanket and, bewildered, she paces back and forth in the dressing room holding it in her arms.

THE LITTLE NEWCOMER

Claes Johansen

Mama was a large and simple woman—we might as well get things above board right from the beginning. She was so huge she could barely edge through a normal doorway. Her looks were terrifying and her language was filthy and sometimes, even at a distance, Mama would scare away small children. She rarely spoke to anyone, more likely she would shout her head off, her hairy upper lip quivering like a little rabbit before the hunter's gun and a tiny mist of spittle always spraying from her lips. But behind all this— her terrible volume, her tone of voice, not to mention a string of invectives that would make a trucker blush— Mama was not at all an unpleasant person. It was just that she had her own rather unfortunate manner, and thinking back I don't believe she ever, in all her lifetime, came close to understanding the impression that she left on others.

Wisely, my sister, Sis, and my brother, Bro, decided to take after Papa, not Mama. In doing so they turned out complete opposites to their mother, Papa being ever so small and cautious a man. Some would go as far as saying that Mama had forced him to marry her. This was not the case. Others would suggest the opposite—that Papa quietly but firmly had forced Mama into their marital union. In fact, only true love had forced them into each other's arms.

Picture Mama standing in the kitchen in all her glory, cooking dinner. She has two huge frying pans going on the gas stove. On one lies a long sausage, spluttering in a spiral. On the other the home-fries are cooking. Above it all the ventilation hood is humming like a giant bumblebee. Now picture the dining room, with Papa, Sis and Bro waiting impatiently. Papa's eyes are glued to the cuckoo clock hanging on the wall above the sofa. See how they all grit their teeth, arms stretched onto the table, fists clenched around knives and forks. Not a word is spoken. Papa prefers to be a man of few words and Sis and Bro, resembling him, and both, well—children of few words!

"Dinner's ready." Mama yells from the kitchen, as if she expects a regiment to line up. Then, carrying the frying pans, she makes her way through the door and into the dining room. Out of breath she moves her mountainous body towards the dinner table. Wham! That was Mama, throwing one frying pan onto the table. And Wham! That was the second one, landing right next to the first.

"There you go, grub's on the table," she yells with the voice of a street singer. "Go, go, go for it—you buggers!"

Sis and Bro remain quiet. They know the rules of this family—wait for Papa to take his food first. So, politely, they wait their turn, while their father carefully cuts himself a piece of sausage.

"Grab a real chunk, now," Mama yells into Papa's face which he has to wipe thoroughly with the cloth serviette before he can finish serving himself.

"'Cause it's fucking great," she says, "and there's tons of it, considering it's you miserable weaklings who're gonna eat it."

Papa doesn't like being called a miserable weakling. So to change the subject of the conversation he says, "How's it going with ... the thing you have in your stomach?"

He covers his mouth with the serviette, stealing a glance at Mama over its edge. Her face—fairly jolly up until now—suddenly turns grey and sad as if Papa's innocent remark has caused her to remember some unhappy event.

"Something wrong?" Papa says.

"I've—ehem—" Mama says, but then her voice drowns out. Never before have Sis and Bro heard her speak at such a low volume.

"The kid slipped right outta me," she suddenly explodes. In the calm after the storm Mama looks at Papa and she looks at her two skinny children, her eyes reflecting both sorrow and regret—though in truth, she has nothing to feel regretful about. It wasn't her fault. It was just one of those things.

"So you actually lost the child?" Papa says, his voice trembling with disbelief and despair. He sits completely still. Slipping off his fork, the large piece of sausage lands on his plate with a splash! A few drops of fat spray up on his white shirt and stain it at the chest, just to the right of his crimson tie.

"It's not true," he says. "Can't be. You're making this up. Please, say you're making this up."

"No, it's the truth," Mama says with a touch of stubbornness in her voice. She doesn't like being called a liar.

"So there I was, just sort of like standing in the fucking shower and out comes this lump. Sliding out of my crotch ever so quietly. I never noticed what happened till there it is, lying there and like plugging up the fucking drain, what with that large funny head and all."

"You must be making this up," Papa says. He doesn't mean that in a literal sense, he just wants to say that this is too awful to be true. But Mama takes everything at face value.

"Better stop saying that all the time, you filthy old man," she says, more injured by the repeated accusation of lying than feeling weighed down by sadness at the un-happy event. Isn't that just like Mama—her moods always changing like the weather in April! Poor Papa, on the other hand, is so affected by the loss that he barely takes notice of Mama as she angrily rises from her chair and disappears in her usual troubled way of walking. Lifting his head, Bro takes a deep breath and is about to say something when Sis, with great sensitivity to the situation, sticks her finger across his lips and whispers, "Shhh!"

She gives Bro a meaningful look and he looks sullen but keeps quiet.

A quick glance at Papa is enough to convince the siblings that the situation requires them to look down, and they stare downwards so intently that they hardly notice what Mama is doing.

She's been in the kitchen, fishing something out of the garbage, and now she returns to the dining room. This something she carries in her right hand—a small bluish body from which she, irritatedly, attempts to shake coffee grounds and potato peels. With the elegance of a weight lifter she reaches the dinner table and the other three family members, sitting with their heads bowed. Quickly, she clears away the salt shaker and the pepper mill and the large frying pan, and "Wham!" That was Mama throwing the curious little body on the dining table.

"There you go, our own little wimp," she yells, but not in an unfriendly tone of voice. This is only Mama being informative. Papa looks up.

"What on earth is that?" he says, frightened, filled with disgust. "Well, it's pretty obvious, isn't it?" Mama says. "If you don't believe what people are telling you you've gotta see for yourself, right?"

Papa mumbles, "It's revolting—and right in the middle of dinner— couldn't you at least have waited till— later?"

Sis and Bro agree.

"This time you've really gone too far, Mama," they say—first Bro, then his sister. With fascinated disgust they look at the earthly remains of the little brother they never had—extending from the navel, a cord stretches across the table and up into the frying pan with the sausage.

"Stinks too," Sis says, as if this being had decided to smell bad just to spite her.

Suddenly, Mama starts laughing. She grabs the little body under its arms and pushes it up under Sis's face and she shakes her large hand to make it look like its body is moving.

"Ooooohh!" Mama yells and Sis squeals like a pig, her hair standing up like the bristles on a hedgehog. Then she starts crying. Casually, and slightly irritated, Mama says, "You always get so excited, Sis. And why all this fuss? Food's gonna go cold." Mama offered to remove the little blue being. But Papa said it didn't matter anymore, he was growing used to it. So they propped it up with its head— much too large—against the wall. Fat from the frying pan dripped from the umbilical cord, making ugly stains on the table cloth, but nobody took any notice.

"He'd be sitting there like that with his tight little limbs."

"Oh yeah!" Bro said with surprising enthusiasm. "Had he not been stillborn he would have thought, 'I've joined a really good family.'"

Sis returned to the table. She had calmed down again. That's how things usually went when Mama did something out of the ordinary—first a huge commotion and, "Really, Mama, this time you've just gone too far," but then everyone would calm down again and things could be dealt with in a more relaxed frame of mind.

"Look at the way he frowns," Sis said. And true enough, the little forehead on the almost spherical head was furrowed by a couple of deep wrinkles, making the little fellow look curiously like an old man. His fingers, also wrinkled, looked like tiny distended sausages being held out in front of his body—and as he sat there with his mouth wide open, he looked quite aggressive as if he had been doing an imitation of a desperate agitator at the moment he had slid out.

"Say 'hello' to little brother," Mama suggested, and though at first Sis would shake her head fervently, she finally reached across the table and said, "Hello," holding the stiff little fingers in her hand.

"He's quite cute, actually," she said, her eyes glistening. Mama nodded with her mouth full of potatoes.

"You just have to get used to him," she said. "It's a pity that the little fool had to be so damned impatient."

"Guess we'll have to give it another try," Papa said, sounding quite cheerful. Mama's face lit up. Papa pushed

—77—

his plate to the side and thoroughly wiped the corners of his mouth.

Indeed, when the family rose from the table the mood was quite good and it got even better later, when they were having their evening coffee. Bro had turned on the radio, now humming in the background. Papa had lit his large meerschaum pipe. The window was open, to let in some fresh air, and from the streets below well-known sounds floated in, mixing with the music from the radio to form a wonderful synthesis.

"Well, yes," said Papa. "I suppose it could have been a lot worse, really." Raising his pipe, he pointed in the direction of the dinner table. "I mean the fact the he never got born. That way he's spared a great deal of trouble."

"Yes, and in a way he got out of having to die again," my sister Sis said.

"That's a lot more than can be said for the rest of us," my brother Bro added.

They all looked over towards the dinner table now, Mama too, and for a moment it seemed as if the little ball of a face gave them a relieved and encouraging smile.

"That's it," said Mama. "That's my big boy."

THE HEIGHTS OF HAPPINESS

Hanne Marie Svendsen

In the small town in the provinces where I grew up there were dance lessons offered for three- to six-year-olds every Thursday in the large room at the hotel. It had the sour and cold smell of a vacant resort hotel. Raised on a platform in a corner a lady with sad eyes sat at the piano and in the middle of the floor stood the instructor counting out the steps 1-2-3, 1-2-3.

I was in love with a boy called Svend, a stocky six-year old powerhouse with an irresistible the-world's-my-oyster look in his eyes. Svend only wanted to dance with Ida, who because of a nervous stomach, spent most of the dance lesson behind the door at the end of the room marked "Ladies". Svend stood in front of that door and bowed while I sent glances thick as caramel towards his turned back.

Only once did I get to dance with Svend. We were doing the rumba when he pushed me so forcefully with his compact behind that I flew diagonally across the room and scraped my shin. I am quite sure that I remember feeling a pang of happiness when I flew across that room. In any event, it was short lived and soon replaced by tears of pain and disappointment.

Tears and dance lessons were connected concepts. At the final concert the youngest girls were to perform a pantomime wearing pink tutus. For the final tableau they all sank down to their knees with their heads back and their small fat arms stretched towards the stucco ceiling—that is, all except me. I stood like a pillar of salt in the middle of the dance floor, tears pouring down my face, until various mothers and aunts saved me from final concerts and all further dance instruction.

When I was fifteen or sixteen it became a burden not

to be able to dance properly. Together with other such misfits I enrolled in an evening course given by an young tradesman who looked like a damp-stained asparagus, spoke in a falsetto voice and whose movements seemed loose and flailing. He was different, subjected to the town's cruel rejection of anyone who was different without being original, and we went to his lessons with feelings of contempt and shame. But here in this ugly dark room he'd been able to rent at the edge of town, our bodies began speaking the right kind of language. When he danced we watched him become beautiful, tight, and concentrated as his eyes grew distant, as if he were in a different world full of joy, togetherness, and acceptance. And slowly we too became less stiff and constrained until one day for a moment we were given entry to his world and were able to touch each other in loving friendship.

This special feeling of happiness, which one can experience in dance, and which I'm trying to get a handle on here, is probably, like so many other things in life, determined by a kind of eroticism. But it was not dependent on the intensity of your feelings toward your dance partner. Of course, you could experience heavenly moments dancing with your current one and only, moments when the narrow space between the two of you was charged with electricity almost visible as little red bolts of lightning. But the dance itself had nothing to do with this feeling of being a two-some. Dance by nature reached outward.

Once a group of students of literature went on a field trip to Uppsala around Valborg Eve. We studied Swedish student life so intensely that most of us fell asleep during the lecture which was our alibi for the trip. For Valborg Eve we were invited to a ball by a students' association. A mountain of a man, a Swede—I barely came up to his shoulders—introduced himself as "the son of a bear hunter from Norrland" and in awe I followed him out onto the dance floor. Once there he behaved exactly as I'd imagined. He mumbled that I must feel squashed down there on the floor so he picked me up and held me on one of his shoulders.

We danced like that for hours, me and the tireless son of a bear hunter. He did all the legwork and I let my entire body move to the rhythm. Others followed his example and up there close to the chandeliers you got the feeling of dancing not just with one person but with the entire room, indeed, to put none too fine a point on it, with the entire universe. While we swung about, our every movement was free, completely free, but at the same time deeply tied to the fellowship of the densely packed dance floor. The glass pearls in the chandeliers sparkled and there was a gleam in everyone's eyes while we swung around in joy and a feeling of belonging together.

The next morning the son of the bear hunter came down to the train station to say good-bye. He brought me a farewell present: a journal of political economy in German, because he had the feeling that I took an interest in languages. I looked at him through the window of my compartment and I thought his face looked like a Camembert cheese. But though the face of the son of the bear hunter quickly erased itself in my mind the sense of having experienced something miraculous stayed with me. It wasn't like the sense of total selflessness as certain mystics have described their climactic experiences. It was rather more a consciousness of individuality and of togetherness, a feeling of being me and at the same time, happily, being a part of humanity.

By definition the indescribable cannot be described. When someone as capable of using the language as Steen Steensen Blicher describes the effect on him of a sunrise over a landscape covered in snow he uses one subordinate clause after another to paint all the colours of morning. But he stops abruptly in front of the main clause which was to describe the climactic moment itself: "But where could be found the mere mortal who possessed the words to capture this the sweetest, the purest of all joys?" Happiness cannot be captured or analysed. It can only be hinted at through suggestive phrases and pictures.

We are dancing together in the sun, mother, three children, a cat and two kittens in the middle of a green lawn, The Beatles playing deafeningly loud on the radio. Our neighbour, an old man, comes in to complain but we take his hand and ask him to join us. And he does, the old man joins us in the sun, dancing to The Beatles on the green lawn.

Or, an official gathering with speeches and formal dress. "My husband can't dance properly at all," a lady states indulgently, after I've been asked to dance and have stood up to walk out onto the floor. And then we begin to jump about without concern for official rules with shrimp-like movements and strange pirouettes creating a perfect rhythm to the point where we communicate like two ex-hibition pilots. And everyone jumps about on the floor in variations never witnessed before. Bow ties go crooked, faces dance behind make-up, the saxophone player swings his instrument and laughs down to us. Somewhere my loved one dances with a beautiful girl in red. They wave, we wave back. Everybody on the dance floor waves and it turns into a variation where we all wave to each other.

Or, a street dance in the old town, where old school mates appear from the darkness. Or, an evening at the cottage with Fats Waller on the turntable and the spicy smell of wet grass while whirling around, dancing not with one person but with everybody in limitless freedom and in a limitless companionship—in a way only experienced in dreams.

And in my dreams I stand inside Copenhagen central station, this sad point of convergence for those who are very lonely and those who are in a hurry. It is winter and dark and the light fixtures cast cones of dull light down over the foreign workers who hang around in the corners, and over all the misfits and the lonely leaning against round tables with nearly empty beer bottles as they seek to make contact. Suddenly a large bronze-coloured man approaches and asks me: "In all the world what is your greatest wish?" He looks like a Buddha who has risen from his lotus position, or the genie in the lamp who has materialized here in Denmark's dark winter. For a second thousands of thoughts cruise through my mind, bits and pieces from political speeches, petitions of solidarity of protest which it was easy to sign because a signature has never been a threat to my own life, feelings of guilt for being a privileged person and protecting my security. Finally, I look straight into the eyes of the bronze-coloured man. Somewhere deep inside I hear a voice remarking with contempt: "You're such a romantic. You're such an escapist. You always take the easy route." But I say it nonetheless: "Imagine if everybody could dance."

"That's a good wish," the genie responds. And immediately the roof of the central station opens up revealing the blue starry sky. Coloured lights descend. They are not attached to anything, they stay afloat by themselves. The mid section of the station with cloakrooms, little shops and lockers is swallowed up into the earth and replaced by a shiny white dance floor. And while the lamps swing, the ceiling ascends, the floor descends and the walls are pushed back, the people begin to dance.

They all dance with refined stylized movements. Pale faces warm up, red noses grow beautiful like gems, every hidden colour of sweater or coat becomes bright in the light. There they all are, known and unknown, an enormous mass of them, as if they were "the great white mass, like a thousand mountains covered in snow", the picture which hung over my great grandmother's bed back home. And on a sign below the orchestra which floats high above on a little white cloud it is written in neat letters: Music of the Spheres.

Then I wake up to the newspapers, headlines and the small and large problems of everyday life. But now and then through the day the feeling suddenly returns, a tight, intense sensation of indescribable happiness, and I say out loud: "Imagine if everybody could dance."

ON THE WAY TO THE CEMETERY

Svend Åge Madsen

It happened just before he reached Ringgaden.

He was aware that he might have been speeding a little but the real problem was that his window wipers didn't quite work. Actually, you could only see lights through his windshield, unlit objects were invisible. But, the police were seldom out this early in the morning.

There was an eerie thunk and the car gave a jerk. Something hit the windshield. He didn't know how but he managed to stop the car almost right on the spot. Something was terribly wrong. He couldn't feel that immediately. He'd hit his forehead against the windshield; otherwise, he was fine. The windshield was cracked. He knocked on it with his elbow. Once more. Not hard enough. One more time and suddenly he was caught in a small snow-storm of little glass pieces.

He got out.

It was a man. Curiously someone had already placed a bouquet of carnations next to his unmoving body. The body was ...

Everything turned into a movie which didn't seem to have anything to do with him. People came running in slow motion from all sides. They spoke first to him and then to each other when they realized that he wasn't participating. More people arrived. Then an ambulance came which they insisted that he get into instead of the man on the road.

He drank his beer very slowly. He still felt hazy. Not because he had hit his head but from the events of the day.

The police officer who had questioned him had been most understanding. The man had walked out on the street without checking for traffic. On his way to work he had decided to put some flowers on his parents' grave. He wasn't dead—yet. But he would probably never regain consciousness.

He had been allowed to leave the hospital after the questioning. He was in a state of shock and he had a band-aid on his forehead, but otherwise he felt quite like his usual self.

He'd bought a bouquet of carnations and gone to the cemetery. He had taken the time and effort to find the parents' grave. There had been no one else with the name Osgren.

Afterwards he had taken a room at a modest hotel nearby. He couldn't drive on in his car and no one was expecting him. This morning he had risen early again. He had "borrowed" a morning paper from a stack in front of a store. There was an ad for a job in Vejle. He'd packed just the most necessary things and taken off in the hope of being the first person there. He wasn't really sure that he wanted the job but everything would lose its meaning if he didn't keep looking.

After a few more beers he asked to borrow a phone book. He was the only patron in the lounge. The waitress slung it to him in a tired gesture. He was lucky again— there was only one family of that name. The address couldn't be far away as it was located on the street he'd been driving on when ...

It was a one family house set a little back from the street. It looked dark but he got up his courage and proceeded somewhat hesitantly. There was no door bell. As he brought up his hand, perhaps to knock, the door flung open.

In front of him stood a woman. Her coat was half way on. The moment she saw him she froze. Her mouth opened and her bloodshot eyes stared directly at him. He wasn't able to move, either. There was something eerie, hypnotic about her gaze.

Eventually he managed to mumble a few words to the effect that he was the driver and that he was sorry.

He was prepared for many different responses: that she'd slam the door in his face; that she'd chase him away; and, even that she'd tell him off. But he was not prepared for what she did do. Without any warning her hand, with her index finger pointed, shot out towards him, towards his eye. She would probably have poked his eye out if, instinctively, he hadn't turned his head away which resulted in her making a cut with her finger nail under his eye.

She took no notice of the injury she had caused him. She slammed the door behind her and as she put on her coat she ran down the path and got into the taxi which had pulled up outside.

Before he could recover from his astonishment the taxi had disappeared, only to be replaced by a small white car shortly after. A young lady emerged and walked towards him with a five- or six-year-old boy in her hand.

"Well, there you are? We couldn't understand why Henrik didn't get picked up."

"I think his mother is on her way down to get him. Something has happened to ..."

"Goodbye, Henrik. Remind your father you have to be picked up by five thirty ... I have to run."

She disappeared and he was left with a blond little boy whose father he'd just killed. Strangely, the little boy held up his hand as if to hold his. Involuntarily he pulled away his hand and stepped back from the trusting boy.

In order to avoid uncomfortable questions he interrogated the boy thoroughly about his kindergarten, about the teacher who'd dropped him off and about his sister, Helene, who was in grade two. He was so preoccupied with leading the boy away from the inevitable question lurking in the background that he realized too late that the taxi had returned and let the woman out. The black coat fluttering behind her she charged towards them like a courageous female animal attempting to save her young one from a predator. She succeeded in her quest as he quickly retreated, leaving her with her child unharmed. He had prepared a few phrases but they seemed unreasonable to him in the current situation. Before he was able to come up with new words the door had slammed behind the two people seeking safety.

When he woke up in the little hovel it was night-time. A nearly empty bottle was standing on the table. He had a throbbing headache. At the same time he had an uncommonly clear impression of the fact that he was going to die. It wasn't that he was going to die right now, he just experienced very concretely that he wasn't going to live for ever. He found a piece of paper and meticulously he wrote down a few words.

He woke up very late in the morning. On the table lay the empty bottle and a note written with stilted letters which reminded him of experiments he made with his handwriting when he was in school. The words in the note appeared strange and so bombastic they could have made him embarrassed. He crumpled the paper and, since he couldn't find a wastepaper basket, stuffed it into one of the pockets in his briefcase.

The accident was mentioned in two of the morning papers. They both maintained his innocence. The dead man, or rather, the dying man had stepped out in front of the car without checking for traffic.

There was light inside the house but no one seemed to be home. There were no movements, no smoke came from the chimney. Still, he felt pulled towards the front door. He hadn't knocked very hard when the door flung open as it had when he was there last. He half expected that something would jump out at him and poke out his eye.

Since this didn't happen he stepped inside. He

supposed that she'd been in a hurry and hadn't closed the door properly.

The house had a particular smell, a balanced mixture of soap, tobacco and perfume, which set it apart from any other house. A wooden spiral staircase led upstairs. From the dark foyer he walked into the bright living room with many green plants, a few light pieces of furniture in the modern style, and a somewhat fresher smell which indicated that people weren't supposed to smoke in here. He walked around the room aimlessly, following the worn down tracks in the carpet, sitting here and there, looking in the bookcases, and letting his fingers slide down over the smooth surface of the abstract figurines in the windowsill.

A large window faced the well-kept garden. The lawn needed to be mowed, however. Perhaps the dying man had planned to mow it after work. The side window faced a small play area. The children had left a doll and some cars out there.

On the glass table lay an open book. In front of it at an angle stood an armchair, pulled back as if it had suddenly been vacated. It was as if a gust of wind had blown the life out of the house as well as the garden. An eerie sense of power trickled through his being.

The next room was an office. Carefully, he closed the door after him in order not to let the smell of smoke seep into the living room. There was a large old desk with a great deal of neatly stacked papers. Against the end wall stood a sofa with worn plush upholstery. A broad, sunken leather chair took up the rest of the room. A black box contained a directory of customers, and the papers were insurance policies. This room had a completely different feel from the living room. It was small, dense and in use. Paper weight, calculator, telephone. The room was filled but nothing was superfluous. He looked through a calendar with appointments. He closed it when he realized the many plans its owner had for the immediate future.

The window faced the street but the venetian blinds

were drawn. As if by reflex, he took note of where the light switches were placed, which floor boards creaked and he investigated which drawers worked easily and which tended to get stuck. One bookshelf was filled with computer books. On the others there were reference books, dictionaries and an encyclopedia.

He was just looking at some photos on the bulletin board when the front door opened. It would have been useless to try to hide in the small room. He would rather be caught standing in the middle of the room than be caught like a child with his hair sticking up over the desk top.

It had to be her. After a few paces back and forth in the foyer she went into the living room. The carpet in there made it difficult to follow her movements. She sighed several times as if she were about to cry or had cried recently. At one point she came close to the door at the office. She opened a cupboard and took out something that made a clinking sound—a bottle and a glass? Then she moved away.

The photos on the bulletin board were of the family. Some had caught the children playing. The girl bathing a doll on a sunny day in the yard. The boy, Henrik, pretending to fix a bike with its wheels turned up.

It gave him a fright when the chair she was sitting in was forcibly pushed back. She was restless. Again, she gave a heavy suppressed sigh. She walked into the foyer and then up the stairs, which he supposed led to the bedrooms, with heavy slow steps.

He kept looking at the confident smiles on the photos. It would have been impossible to open the door and walk through the foyer without making a noise. He could try to sneak out and risk being caught. He could rush out, which would certainly frighten the woman, alert her, and she would probably recognize him as he ran down the path. Finally, he could wait and see what would happen. Deep in thought he took a pipe from the rack and tested it by putting it in his mouth. Against all common sense he slipped into the chair which creaked under him. Hopefully the sound couldn't be heard upstairs.

The steps on the staircase surprised him. They were different from the earlier ones. She must have changed her shoes. She'd probably gone upstairs to get changed. She walked into the living room.

Suddenly a voice spoke right into his ear. He gave a fright. The voice disappeared again in the middle of a word. Then it returned and disappeared just as abruptly again. It continued in the living room. She had turned off the speaker in the office. The news was on. She turned it off when the weather report started.

He became infected by her restlessness but he had little room to move in. He began to pace the length of the room avoiding the floor boards that creaked.

"Is anyone here?" She suddenly called out from the living room.

He froze. She mumbled to herself in order to talk herself out of the idea, or, to build up enough courage to go and check. He held his breath.

"No, no, no," she said. This time nearer the door to the office. "Michael," she mumbled. "Oh, Michael."

Over and over she moaned the dying man's name "Michael."

As if she were conjuring him back.

"Michael, Michael."

As if she could hold on to him by clinging to his name.

"Michael, no."

As if she blamed him for leaving her.

He had to clench his teeth in order not to answer her plea for help. He pressed his hands against his ears.

The sharp ringing finally stopped her moaning. The telephone! On the desk. He reached for it to disconnect the sound. Quickly he pulled back his hand. He was caught in a trap. He was afraid of being exposed but he was upset at the thought of her fear when she'd come in and face him.

Her horror at ...

The ringing stopped. She answered loudly, quickly. She had answered the phone in the living room. Her voice became hesitant. Then it became weak to the point of disappearing.

"Yes ... Yes ... I'll be there ..."

She put down the phone. Her breathing was deep and erratic. Then she dialled a number and asked for a taxi to come as soon as possible.

She paced frantically in the foyer before she left the house. The door slammed behind her.

He waited till he was certain the taxi had picked her up before he left the house. The door slammed behind him.

He noticed the vague contours of his reflection in front of him. It looked odd, as if the man in the image was disappearing. Confused, he let his gaze drop to the meaningless goods displayed in the store window.

When he looked back up the situation hadn't improved. The people in the pedestrian street were clearly reflected in the window but the light prevented him from seeing himself.

On a sudden impulse he went into a barber's for a shave and a trim. His reflection in the mirror was bright and clear.

Before closing time he was standing on the side walk across from the kindergarten. The same woman he'd seen the day before emerged holding Henrik by the hand. He hurried over to them. The woman didn't say a word to him. She just let go of Henrik and pushed him in the direction of the approaching man.

The boy seemed a little more hesitant than the previous day but they walked together to his home without his asking questions about his absent father.

He would have let Henrik knock on the door and then leave when he saw that the boy was safely at home.

But, contrary to his plans the boy tore himself free and rushed into the house. He stood indecisively outside the door. He couldn't leave the boy alone. He had to make sure that someone was at home.

No one answered his knock so he built up his courage to walk into the foyer. He reached the entrance to the living room. The woman who was sitting with her son gave a fright.

"Mommy's crying." He mumbled an apology but before he managed to withdraw Henrik had run up to him.

"I'll get Helene," the boy said and continued on into the foyer and up the stairs.

"Michael is dead," the woman said when the boy was out of earshot. "I have no one ... Would you be kind enough to get the kids started on a game before you leave? ... Please, don't tell them ..."

He nodded and withdrew before she gave in to her sorrow. He caught the children on the stairs and managed to convince them to go back to their room upstairs. It was simple enough to get them started playing but every time he was about to leave they threatened to follow him downstairs.

This was repeated several times. Helene had staring eyes. She was skinny and seemed restless as if she sensed what had happened.

After he had read a story to them and had got them involved in drawing they let him go downstairs on the condition that he would return.

Their mother had pulled herself together. Her eyes were as penetrating as her daughter's.

"I must apologize," she said. "Their grandfather, my husband's father, died a short while back. Helene was completely floored by it. I don't dare tell her that ..."

She started to cry again. There was something disconcerting about her. Her features were sharp, her nose a little large, and her hair was combed tightly back. She was bent over slightly like a taut spring. Anni was her name.

He'd seen her name in the phone book.

"I promised the kids to come back up. I can put them to bed in a while."

"That would be a great help. I really don't know what to do ..."

After he had entertained the children for a while they wanted something to eat before going to bed. He sneaked downstairs. When he saw their mother sitting engrossed in her sorrow he stole out to the kitchen without saying a word. He fried some potatoes and heated up the leftovers he could find. He gave a serving to the woman, along with a short explanation, before he went back upstairs to the children with their food. After he had read them a chapter from the book they'd started they accepted that it was bed time.

Anni sat in the same position. He pressured her to eat a little of the meal which had turned cold. She mumbled something, as if she wasn't aware that he was in the room.

"I don't understand... Michael ... It's as if he were still here ... It feels so unreal ..."

He convinced her to go up and rest. She was so weak that her legs gave in and he had to support her up the stairs. She lay down with her clothes on. When he was about to leave he caught some of what she was saying, as if it were directed to herself.

"I'm afraid of how Helene will react ... I'm afraid that she'll get ill. When I tell her tomorrow ..."

"I could come and take them to school and to kindergarten," he offered, partially because he was also concerned about how their mother would cope.

She barely responded but he thought he noticed her nod to him.

As he was about to leave with the children the next morning a man came to the house. He said his name was Knud Monikke and he asked if he might return after the kids were in school so they could have a talk, undisturbed.

The man said that he was the psychiatrist who had tended to Helene after her grandfather's death. He was very concerned about her. He could not vouch for her reaction to being told of her father's death right now, as she was quite unprepared.

Anni begged him for something to calm herself. The psychiatrist, however, didn't think that mourning was something to suppress but rather something to be treated by talking through it. Only by talking thoroughly about one's relationships and feelings was it possible in the long run to fill the vacuum in life which had suddenly appeared. When Anni explained that she didn't have any family, just a few acquaintances who were much too absorbed in their own lives, the psychiatrist turned meaningfully towards him. Consequently, he felt obliged to offer to stay and talk to the woman, which was accepted.

When Monikke had left they sat uncomfortably across from one another but after a while he succeeded in getting her to talk. At first she was hesitant but eventually she discovered that her guest was listening with genuine interest and her descriptions became more lively. One memory brought another along and emotions she had hardly verbalized before appeared in her conversation.

Michael, her husband, had been a very warm and energetic man when he was with the children. With strangers he often seemed reserved but he was always reliable. Way back when he first met Anni he had been possessed by her. Rather than simply falling in love with her, he'd been overtaken by an emotion whose power had taken him by surprise. Still, after ten years of marriage he was sometimes frightened by his lack of self-control in his relationship with her.

She talked about this and that. She even followed him and kept talking when he went into the kitchen to make them a few sandwiches. It was as if, in the course of the day, she had to look into her life in a deeper context than she ever had before and she finished by whispering thoughtfully to herself: "I don't want to lose it. I don't want to lose it."

After he had picked up the children, occupied them a little, and put them to bed, she said to him, frightened: "This may sound strange, but I fear for myself. Last night ... I don't know what I might do."

"If it would be helpful I can stay the night," he offered. "I could sleep in there on the sofa."

She felt so relieved by his offer that it didn't occur to her that it was strange that he knew the layout of the house.

"That's really kind of you. Just this first night. It's so awful when I'm alone. I hear voices, I feel his presence in the house, I think I can hear his footsteps. Last night ... I thought I was going mad."

When he was lying on the sofa he couldn't fall asleep. He tried not to move in order not to frighten or wake up Anni. Finally he pulled out the most elementary of the computer books from the shelf. It was a subject which had never interested him in the least and it took a great deal of effort for him to get into it, but eventually he found it easier.

The book lay by his side and the lamp was on when he woke up in the middle of the night. He had fallen asleep with the light on, something he'd never done before.

But now he was unable to fall back to sleep. He lay there thinking about what Anni had told him the previous day while he conjured up her penetrating eyes and her chiselled profile. He thought about the desire which had possessed the man he had killed.

The next day there were quite a few things which had to be arranged in connection with the death, and since Anni appeared to be hopeless and uncertain he presented himself as effective and resolute in order to calm her. Though it was quite a new experience for him to behave in this manner he quickly learned how easy it actually was to take charge and settle firmly on any random possibility.

On the other hand, he felt he had to strain to appear inventive and lively for the children who by now knew all the entertainment possibilities he normally sought recourse in. But through deep concentration he managed after all to invent some games which completely absorbed them.

Later that day he confided his observation to Anni: "It's strange. To be decisive involves choosing without thinking. To be spontaneous and energetic involves long and careful consideration."

Anni looked at him and pondered. "That's exactly the kind of thing Michael would have come up with."

She'd slept soundly the previous night but she had dreamt continuously, as if the tape with her memories had kept playing. He explained to her that this was a sign that she wasn't finished talking. But she didn't feel like continuing even though he encouraged her. Instead she began to talk about the children, about who they really were and about their difficulties, about their funny reactions and subtle replies on various occasions.

She had calmed down and she didn't think he had to sleep over again. But when he explained that he wasn't giving up anything, she let him convince her that he should stay. Besides, she had to admit that it would be easier for her if she didn't have to face the children alone the next morning.

Late that evening he was reading the book he'd begun the night before. There were a number of expressions which were difficult for him to decipher but he made the effort to look them up and make a list of them. This procedure quickly paid off. He enjoyed the discovery that he was actually able to penetrate the demanding text as long as he was sufficiently determined. This insight made him decide to keep even more systematic and thorough notes.

Nonetheless, he finally ran into a technical description he was unable to decipher. This annoyed him. He paced up and down the office for a while and then he sat down at the desk. Deep in his thoughts he opened and closed the drawers until he caught sight of a stack of papers. He pulled them out. On them were notes exactly like the ones he'd begun making. Michael had used the same technique. He too, though he seemed so clear-headed and smart, had found the books difficult. Leafing through the notes he was even able to find the notes belonging to the book he was reading himself. Michael had clearly been stopped in the very same spot but he had found an explanation in another book which had got him out of the conundrum. By following Michael's notes he, too, succeeded in solving the problem.

When he was too tired to read anymore but still not tired enough to sleep he started to play around with the tape recorder. He had also fiddled with it earlier in the evening in order to learn how it worked. Now he realized that he had happened to record most of Anni's talk about the children.

He lay down with the headphones and started the tape from the beginning. Half asleep he heard her magnetic voice talk about the children. Soon his dream visions mixed in with the story. He saw Anni at the beach together with the children. He heard her muffled laughter as the ball hit the strange man.

He woke up feeling as if he had participated in the events Anni had talked about.

He hadn't any clean clothes with him but with Anni's help he found some that Michael had grown too heavy for but which he could just fit into. "You should try to comb your hair down across you forehead and let the hair on your sides come forward in front of your ears," she said as she looked him over. "I could style it a little for you," she offered when he, just for the fun of it, brushed his hair forward as she had suggested.

"I always cut Michael's hair," she added when she

corrected his bangs. "It would suit you to grow it a little longer."

That night they shared a bottle of red wine. He actually preferred beer but he liked the wine because she taught him to drink it with slow probing. They were drinking a wine she and Michael had discovered on a trip to France. Since then they had imported it themselves.

She showed him family pictures. As they looked through them he told her that he had taken quite a few pictures himself. But, when Anni confided to him that Michael didn't like to take the pictures himself he had to admit that he too had lost his interest in photography.

"Michael used to feel that he was uninvolved when he took pictures. That the experience became phoney if he was holding a camera between himself and whatever was going on," she explained.

At that moment he felt a powerful desire to put his arm around her. He started to shiver and sweat sprang forth on his forehead as he tried to suppress his impulse. He jumped up and went to the washroom without an explanation. Only after the pressure had subsided did he return.

"You shouldn't only read those boring textbooks," she said one day. "Michael used to read the novels I liked best. It was really nice to be able to discuss them afterwards."

He explained that he didn't find the textbooks boring at all. The more he got into them, assisted by Michael's notes, the more interesting and lively he found the topic. Apparently Michael had said something similar, but all the same, he did accept the novel she had just finished reading.

One day he took the train back to Viborg. He packed a few things from his bachelor apartment on which he had given notice.

When he returned and stepped into the house there was a strange woman in the living room. She started when she saw him. She turned to Anni.

"Amazing... I didn't know that Michael had a brother."

She turned out to be a cousin of Anni's who was passing through town. While Anni was briefly out of the room she said: "She's taking her loss better than I'd expected."

"Her loss," he said, slightly hurt.

"Yes, Michael meant everything to her."

Then she began to talk about how she'd got along with Michael.

"I'm not interested!" He interrupted her. "I'm not interested in your Michael. I'm only interested in hers."

"I'm sorry, I forgot that you too had lost...," she said. "You're just like your brother, testy and friendly at the same time."

When her cousin had left Anni found the mix up amusing.

"She thought you were your brother," she said by mistake.

In order to hide her confusion she added: "I've told you a lot about me. Tell me about yourself."

It was evident that she'd regretted the suggestion as soon as she'd made it. "There isn't that much to tell. I've always valued my freedom. As a consequence I've been all over the place, never settling down to anything ... never becoming anything."

As he walked through the office building he felt a certain nervousness. He'd been in similar situations several times and he'd always been calm and collected.

Anni's directions led him through several corridors to the right office.

"I'm Jørgen Fegge-Hansen," the middle-aged man behind the desk said. His posture was erect; he was well-dressed and aloof.

"Mrs. Osgren suggested that I come to see you

concerning the position left vacant by Michael Osgren's death. Mrs. Osgren thought that you might be interested in hiring me."

"I don't know how she could have thought that. Besides, the position hasn't even been posted yet."

"I have certain qualifications."

"I'm sure you do. So do many others."

"I'm in the process of improving mine."

"In what way?"

"I have access to Mr. Osgren's notes and so I've been able to familiarize myself with how things work around here."

His words had a surprisingly positive effect. Not that the man had seemed uncomfortable before but all of a sudden he was ready to negotiate.

"I see. Marianne will you get us a cup of coffee?"

His secretary, who was working next to a filing cabinet at the far end of the room, seemed puzzled.

"It's only two o'clock. Mr. Fegge-Hansen."

"Yes. I think I'm getting a sore throat. A cup of coffee would be soothing... Rules are there to be broken."

When the secretary had left the office manager said: "There's a rather touchy matter about the insurance."

"The insurance?"

"Mr. Osgren's life insurance. On one hand we would naturally not want to overrule one of our own employees. On the other, Mr. Osgren didn't actually manage to make his first payment and the insurance is therefore, strictly speaking, not valid. I realize that this puts Mrs. Osgren in a difficult position."

"Mr. Osgren's father died..."

"Yes, I know. It was, in fact, my suggestion that he wait until all the trouble was over. I must admit that I feel quite responsible because of that. Legally speaking I'm in the right, but ..."

"If I assumed Mr. Osgren's position Mrs. Osgren would benefit from my salary and her difficulties would diminish considerably."

"I see. And the insurance might not be claimed in that case?"

"Perhaps the policy could be transferred to cover me. Or, better yet, I could be recorded as Mr. Osgren."

"That's a possibility. It would certainly simplify things. You would simply take over Mr. Osgren's number."

"You mean his personnel number?"

"Indeed. His employment here is still registered as active. So technically speaking, he isn't dead yet. If you take over his number you may step right into his position. The computer can't tell the difference, after all. As soon as you've made the first payment on the policy it comes into effect."

"Sounds simple enough."

"I will look after the necessary adjustments. Our company will go a long way to keep a valued employee."

He didn't find the job all that easy. There were so many new things to get used to. When he returned home after his second day he collapsed in front of the T.V.

"You'll be fine," she said, comforting him. "You'll soon be into the routine."

He shivered but she didn't notice because she was pouring him a glass of wine. She knew what he needed to relax.

They watched a movie for a while then they agreed to turn it off.

"I couldn't stand that last scene," she said. "If there's something I can't stand that's it."

He hadn't noticed anything in particular and asked her to explain.

"The way the big strong hero walks up to the resisting girl. Even though she resists he kisses her. And slowly she turns soft, gives in and receives him eagerly because his kiss is so irresistible. That shows the worst kind of misogyny. As if a woman were nothing but a lump of clay in the hands of a man."

Deep in thought he had picked up the camera from the coffee table in front of him. Excited and with her fiery eyes she made a great picture. While he talked he watched her in the viewfinder. Dizzy, he quickly removed the camera again. He suddenly felt that she, and consequently the whole world, had turned into a movie which was being played out in front of him.

Finally one evening she said: "You can love me now."

"I already do."

She smiled and he could see that he had answered correctly.

"But do you love me enough?" she continued.

"I want you. I want you so badly it feels like I'm gonna explode."

From her subtle nod he could tell that he answered as expected.

Then she said: "What are you going to do about it?"

He got up. Grabbing her supple body, he tore off her dress and entered her with frightening intensity. When he came he felt completely relieved, as if he'd just passed an examination.

After that day he moved into the bedroom. He assumed their family name since three of them had already become used to that. In addition, the children had begun, without encouragement, to call him "dad".

He did his job conscientiously and soon the suspicion he'd felt coming from his superior, the office manager, disappeared. The novels he read mainly out of duty but he enjoyed the conversations they produced.

One day at the cemetery his mouth opened wide and he started to scream as loudly and as intensely as he could. After he'd released the scream he bent down over the grave and made room for the bouquet he had brought. He noticed that the scream had attracted some people but when they saw him, unaffected, pottering about at the grave they felt uncertain and withdrew.

He checked very carefully for traffic before he crossed the road on his way home.

TO WISH FOR A SUDDEN CHANGE

Dorrit Willumsen

*to wish for a sudden
change*

On the playground the girls are walking around in a circle.
They are singing. Their teacher leads the singing and she is
the one who decides whether they should walk fast or slow
and how they should move their arms. Her voice is very
loud. Her hair is blond, her cheeks are flabby and her lips
are deep red. Now and then she smiles. The smile floats
from her mouth over to the row of mothers sitting on the
bench.

In particular, the teacher decides who gets to wear
the veil and the two small crowns made out of wire and
paper flowers. Sleeping Beauty's is red. The one for the
Wise Woman is yellow. These crowns turn the girls into
princesses. Suddenly they're in the middle of the circle.
The others walk around them, singing. The song and the
ways the children in the circle look at them add a graceful
touch to their movements.

One of the girls in the circle has a very bad case of
knock-knees. The tips of her shoes are worn down and she
has decorated her hair with an elastic band. Her hands are
sweaty and every time the song stops she shivers with
excitement because she hasn't yet been chosen. But she
knows that at the very moment she can feel the wire on top
of her head and the elastic band cutting its way under her
chin she will start to move like an elegant lady in a night-
gown. She walks in the circle for that very reason. She
thinks of nothing else.

Abruptly the girls let go of her hand. For a moment
she thinks it's her turn. But, instead, the teacher explains,
slurring her words, a completely different game in which

you're a little green frog. The girl looks at her feet. The sun is beating down hard on the asphalt making it smell like tar. It feels like everything will come apart.

Suddenly she starts to jump and she turns green. Her elastic band is green. She is the greenest of them all. She bends her legs till she's almost crouching and jumps into the air. Very high. Her legs are sturdy frog legs that send her up to the sky. She jumps about and her voice is light and sharp when she yells that she is the frog.

Finally, she grows tired. She sits on the ground and catches her breath. The rest have all disappeared. The teacher, the crowns, the girls and the row of soft, smiling mothers.

The seesaw is reaching towards the tall poplars. The swings hang loosely in their chains. And in the sand boxes the castles stand empty behind their moats filled with forbidden water.

Maybe they all laughed. Maybe the teacher didn't notice her at all and just mumbled something about "next time".

The frog seeps out of the girl's legs. She feels embarrassed and depressed. Knock-kneed, she walks home with small steps. She tries to get the elastic band out of her hair.

never daring to admit
to a dream

The young girl in the butcher shop doesn't know which of her customers is admiring her thighs from a near-by phone booth. He always puts a handkerchief over the mouthpiece.

"One night I'll come to you wearing a black mask," he whispers. "Don't open your eyes, then. Keep on your stockings. And a pair of black gloves. And I will force my way up between your thighs."

The girl slams down the phone and walks out to the

shop to cut herself a piece of the red salami which tastes like dried tears. The white smock makes her look pale. The gliding motion of her hips under the material feels like quick, fluttering caresses.

Perhaps it's the young man with the coveralls and the beautiful dark hair. He orders four open-faced sandwiches every day.

Perhaps it's the man with the heavy bloated face. Roast beef with remoulade sauce and fried onions. Camembert.

Perhaps it's the very old man who buys liver paté for his wire-haired fox terrier.

Or, perhaps she's never even seen him. Perhaps he watches her movements through binoculars from a hallway window in an apartment building.

When she hangs up the phone too fast for him he smothers cream puffs all over the window. She assumes the responsibility of cleaning it. Perhaps he's watching her while she does it.

Anonymously, she thinks. The word is sharp and shines like a stiletto. She doesn't dare to go out after dark any longer. She has bought a safety chain for her door. She hasn't put it on yet. It would be much too conspicuous.

On the bus on her way home she stands, her eyes alert. While her body sways back and forth her mind registers the face of everyone around her. They appear like spots in a pattern of which she's unable to get an overview. She disappears into it.

In her kitchen she quickly puts on water for tea. She eats three hard boiled eggs and some shrimp from the shop which they would have thrown out in any case because of the expiry date.

In the middle of the night she wakes up and thinks about the voice which sweeps down over the raw filet and the big bowls filled with sauces and mayonnaise and into her ear. And she can't breathe.

"It's a nightmare," she thinks. "My blood is turning

into ice."

She presses her forehead against the window and finds it odd that her skin feels so hot.

to see yourself as the image
of another

She's standing in the kitchen. The linoleum on the counter is so new that it still smells slightly chemical. It doesn't have a single scratch yet. And she is careful not to leave any spots when she unwraps the fish.

Cross-eyed, the flounder looks up at her with a little malevolent smile. The white paper surrounding it looks like thin drenched silk. The wedding announcements on the newspaper wrapping give her a gentle shock.

She and her husband are almost dissolved by the liquid from the fish. She's standing there with some kind of crown on her head made from white tulle folded into a flower. The veil is close to her cheeks. The white surface of the dress has erased her body. Next to her he stands like a dark statue. It's the same photo they have on the wall. Both pictures show a cool smooth sheen where once sweat had glistened on their temples. Their nervousness had condensed into large smiles which now almost rise up through the surface of the picture to announce their happiness.

Carefully, she scrapes off the small, hard scales from the picture. She looks at it for a long time. Before she throws it out she presses her lips against it. It tastes like a salty underwater kiss and she doesn't know whether she kisses him or herself.

She walks out to the mirror in the foyer and looks at her face. Her reflection is clear, sharp and serious. She closes her eyes a little and parts her lips slightly. Then she bends her neck backwards and tries to see herself through his eyes until her reflection disappears from sight and she becomes dizzy.

She straightens herself quickly as if she'd been caught doing something she wasn't supposed to do.

She walks back to the kitchen and begins to scale the fish with short, quick strokes.

Maybe she'll mention seeing the picture to him. But she's not certain that it is funny. She can't get it to hang together as a story. When he tells her something she knows precisely when to laugh.

She has his name. And when someone calls her "Mrs." she straightens a little and smiles.

to be far removed from the signals of
your body

She's lying in a white bed. The whole room is white. Even the sounds seem buffered by white felt in order not to disturb her. Her body no longer belongs to her. It's inhabited by a child. And she's not made for it. She doesn't have the sense of inner joy pregnant women should feel.

During pre-natal classes she sighed and she's been known to use her large grey coat as camouflage by closing every button in it. Now she's lying quietly eating an egg without salt because of the baby. She opens the shell with small soft movements as if she were committing a crime. She swallows her pills unquestioningly and she feels guilty about her un-cooperative body and the dark heaviness of her blood.

When they ask how she feels she answers politely that she's fine and wonders why they seem to expect her to say something different.

She no longer remembers what exactly she has in her purse. She looks over towards the window as if she were able to draw the coolness of the window pane down on her face. Without raising her head she combs her hair.

A young plump nurse enters, moving like an excited kitten.

—109—

"Things will appear a little hazy now," she says and holds up the pipette.

The eye drops hit her like a stinging rain. Though she is afraid, her lips form some kind of smile as the nurse's pretty red mouth sails away and the contours of her purse disappear.

Like the Flying Dutchman the ophthalmologist appears in the fog. He bends in over her to look into her eyes, his fingers resting lightly against her cheekbones.

"No improvement," he sighs. "Take care."

"And you," she mumbles and then she registers a subtle shiver moving through his body as if she had pulled an electric switch.

He has left and she thinks about her medicare card in her purse and the child in her stomach. When she's asked if she looks forward to being a mother she says yes, though she's not quite sure.

Her husband's sweaters shine brightly. He visits wearing his faded green, his bronze or his light blue sweater. Soft spots of colour in the fog.

Sometimes she can tell that he's been drinking.

The flowers on her table slowly suck up the water.

Needles slowly suck her blood and her urine needed for analysis.

When the closet, her purse and the flowers regain their solid contours she tries to read.

She's reading Malinovski's *Poetomatic*:

notice
the walnut's little brain
and
spare at least it

As long as they put the child into a little white cot they can do whatever they have to do to her body.

Suddenly, she recalls seeing her own x-ray. Her bones looked peculiarly slim and beautiful. Only the lead seal shone incompletely through the white flower-shape in her cranium.

The doctor enters abruptly with two nurses and a midwife. They tie the blood pressure cuff around her arm. They listen for the child and ask her if she'd mind if they gave her a Caesarean section.

"No," she answers overwhelmed, "not if you really want to go to all the trouble."

She doesn't comprehend their laughter which bounces around the room like little pearls.

They give her a pill so that they can take her blood pressure every half hour without waking her up.

A dark-headed nurse shaves off her pubic hair. She thinks about the brutality of that concept as compared to the mildness she sees in the woman's face. Other than that she feels as if she were floating outside herself.

The next morning she takes the book out from the drawer again. The light is dim and grey.

"Whistling is prohibited in the General Savings Bank."

She doesn't get further than that because an attendant suddenly takes the book from her explaining to her in a slight Bornholm-dialect that she shouldn't be reading. Books can be subversive and according to him one should admire athletes.

For the moment she floats in the air in a state of wonderment. But soon enough the elevator sucks them down to the bottom while the uniformed man with beautiful blue eyes explains in his equanimous voice that he's a fan of Mohammed Ali and that he also admired him as Cassius Clay.

He fills up her mind with sweat, ice water and white towels.

"And athletes don't smoke," he says.

"No." She hears her own voice flap about in the elevator sounding like that of a young girl, as light as a bird.

Mohammed Ali has never smoked. Not when he was Cassius Clay, either.

She closes her eyes and thinks about beautiful blue butterflies and what it would be like to smoke a cigarette right now.

She wants to tell the porter that she agrees. But when she opens her eyes he is gone and she is parked outside a kiosk exhibiting tiny scissors.

A blond woman smiles soothingly.

"You won't even remember if it's a boy or a girl when you come back out. You will keep asking."

She's pushed past the kiosk and suddenly she lies very high up hovering between people wearing half-masks and the shiny helmet covering the lights. She feels as if her body has turned into a much too small and hilly terrain which has suddenly become the object of a military campaign.

"Have you been catheterised?"

The voice is very clear and close to her ear.

"Sorry, I don't understand."

"Has your urine been drained?"

She shakes her head which simultaneously disappears into a hood as if she were now one of them.

"She doesn't need an anaesthetic for that."

She feels a small, cool and light pain.

It feels quite sharp and it vibrates like an arrow. A clear and worried voice says: "Blood pressure at 210."

"We don't believe that. Let's begin." It is the doctor's voice overriding the reading.

"Oxygen," another voice tempts softly.

Dizzy, she inhales.

"Will this child ever be able to whistle?"

a movement which wipes out
a face

His foot wakes her up. It makes an intimate, demanding motion against her calf. Sleep still clinging to her eyelids she feels his member against her lips.

"Why?" she mumbles. The pressure on her mouth forces open her jaw.

"Quick," she thinks, "quick and easy."

"Is this love?" She moves her tongue.

"Or hate?" She bends backwards to catch her breath. His skin is warm and it thumps.

"Desire," she thinks. "Not for me, perhaps not for anyone in particular."

She feels the pressure of his member against her lips and in her mouth and she senses a vacancy in her body.

After the child left her body her breasts started to sag. Her stomach pulled back in like a boy's. And her legs, though they stayed thin, no longer had the nimbleness of the young animal. An awkward stiffness settled into her limbs.

She closes her eyes tightly to think about something else.

"Touch me," he whispers.

She sighs and she knows that he can tell it isn't a sigh of pleasure. It is a relinquishing sigh. He would call it a cold sigh.

His skin has a slight odour of alcohol and sweat and she tries to think about the ocean, plains and forests. Behind her closed eyes she tries to conjure up pictures of landscapes she has never seen while his hands close more and more tightly around her cheeks.

"You're like a hare," he once said, because of her shyness.

Suddenly she recalls a passage from her cookbook: it is easy to tear the ears off a young hare. It is more difficult to do so on an old hare. The skin at the corners of the eyes

—113—

is soft on the young hare. On an old hare the areas around the eyes and the nose are hard. Hard.

Her eyes sting. The fur of the hare. Her hands are cupped around his testicles. She no longer tries to caress him, rather, she's trying to push him away. He gives up and turns over. Shortly after he's asleep, or he's pretending to be asleep.

She wants to get up silently and put on her black lace negligee and wear it against her skin as a sign of mourning. And her beautiful golden cotton coat with the torn lining. Then her long lined gloves so she'll look like a lady after all. And her white boots which make her gait smooth.

She wants to walk straight ahead and not meet anyone she knows.

Ahead of her lies the possibility of change. Behind her all the nights when they gave up on each other.

The days when they were planning their silver anniversary. Her menstruation at forty-five which wouldn't end. And the beautiful woman doctor who observed the stream of blood with a lamp on her forehead like a miner or a fairy. The days when she smelled like she had died before her time. He reproached her for the fear which seeped through her skin and her perfume. And she realized that she'd turned into a grey spot in a picture she no longer recognized.

For a moment she tenses her body and feels a sharp sense of hatred.

But then, abruptly, she begins to think about the days when they both believed that they could live normally and happily together.

Those days and the innocent blue skies which overarched everything else.

With her pillow she seals her mouth.

to keep a secret
when you're lost

The old woman lies under a baby blue comforter and stares into an off-white wall. She doesn't remember how old she is any longer. Sometimes they call her by the wrong name and she gently shakes her head. But it doesn't make any difference.

Some days she sees the faces of dead relatives in the living ones and she tries to call them by name, like a child braiding a brittle wreath. When they reveal the betrayal to her everything crumbles. And she turns back towards the wall and feels the pain sink down, settling into her loose skin which is much too large.

Sometimes a fleeting scent of flowers will make her recall the pink, blue and yellow pieces of soap which used to slide through her hands when she worked at the factory.

The soap was smooth and fine. It felt strangely alive when she picked it off the assembly line to wrap it. Then her hands would fold the sky blue tissue paper into pleats held together with pink tape and rosettes.

She was a fast worker back then. The fastest and the most accurate of them all. Her superiors valued her and gave her a dog in Royal Copenhagen. But things are different now.

Now her body is immovable and soft and the temperature of her skin changes after her room has been aired out. They pick her up and put her in bed. They unwrap her and wrap her.

She tries to imagine her body as a yellow piece of soap. But from the touch of their hands she can tell that the comparison doesn't work. Soap is smooth and fine. Immovability is the only thing she shares with it. Her thoughts crumble.

One day they pick her up gently and they carefully mention her name while they support her body with pillows.

They tell her it's her birthday and that she'll have visitors. They comb her hair painstakingly as if they're unable to do it well enough, though she struggles to keep her head straight.

A young girl bends down towards her in a friendly manner. She is holding a small box with red and blue colours in her hand. The old woman remembers the cheap water-colours the kids used to smudge all over the paper, and she smiles.

The young girl takes the smile for a yes and she bends down over her face.

With able hands she paints a pair of light blue wing shapes on the old woman's eyelids, then she puts a pink spot on each of her cheeks and paints a tiny red mouth on the loose lips.

"You look really nice now," she chirps.

Her hand is too heavy to reach her face.

"You're barely recognizable..."

And as if in a very clear light the old woman suddenly sees her brother and her niece approach between the rows of beds.

They peek over all the sky-blue comforters as they move slowly and gently like two angels carrying fragile bouquets in their hands.

The old woman flashes a raspberry red smile at them. She can tell that they don't recognize her. But she doesn't give it away. She keeps it secret when they finally hold out their hands to her and she feels that a real change could occur any time now.

BENNY ANDERSEN (b. 1929) left public school after grade seven shortly after which he continued his education at night school while apprenticing at an advertising company. He completed Gymnasium in 1948. Having grown up in a musical household, he travelled Scandinavia as a musician from 1949 to 1962. He visited New York in 1956 and 1958 while playing on Norwegian cruise ships. He began writing while he was a musician and he made his literary debut in 1960 with the poetry collection *Den Musikalske Ål* [The Musical Eel] and he has since published over 30 books in poetry, short stories, novels, children's books, songs and play scripts. He has also written drama for stage, radio, television and the screen. His work has been translated into English *(Selected Poems, Selected Stories,* and *The Pillows),* German, French, Italian, Swedish, Russian and Czech. "A Happy Time" was first published in his collection of stories *Over Skulderen* [Over the Shoulder] in 1983.

JYTTE BORBERG (b. 1917) made her debut in 1968 with her collection of short stories *Vindebroen* [The Drawbridge] and her first novel *Nældefeber* [Nettle Rash] appeared in 1970. During the '70s and '80s Jytte Borberg added well over twenty titles to her *oeuvre.* She has also written drama for the stage, radio and television. She lives in the village of Fjaltring (which is also the home of Tukak' Teatret, a theatre she enjoys very close contact with) right by the North Sea. "Do Not Cross the Tracks" first appeared in the collection *Suset* [The Whoosh], published in celebration of her seventieth birthday, in 1987.

BO GREEN JENSEN (b. 1955) is a writer, critic and lecturer. He has written twenty-five books since 1981, including novels, poetry, short stories, and collections of essays on literature, music and film. He spent two years in the U.S. as a Visiting Fellow in American Studies at Yale University and as a Writer-in-Residence at the University of Minnesota. His work has been translated into English, German, French, Hebrew, Swedish, Norwegian, and Icelandic. He lives in Copenhagen and works as a literary critic at a weekly newspaper. "A Place to be Human" was first published in Politiken in 1990.

ULLA RYUM (b. 1937) made her debut in 1962 with the novel *Spejl* [Mirror]. Since then she has published collections of short stories, novels and plays. She is also very active as a stage director of her own plays which have been performed in regional theatres as well as the Royal Theatre in Copenhagen. Her work as a dramaturge takes her all over the Nordic countries where she frequently works with marginalized cultural groups such as the Sami and the Faroe Islanders. She recently won the Holberg Prize, one of the highest honours a dramatist can receive in Denmark. "One of the Little Saviours" was first published in Politiken in 1988.

NIELS HAV (b. 1949) made his debut with the story collection, *Afmægtighed forbudt* [Powerlessness Forbidden]. Since then he has published several collections of poems and short stories as well as two novels. He has studied theology and he has been employed as a hotel porter, a sand blaster, a gardener and as a land surveyor. Now a full-time writer he was awarded a three-year grant from Statens Kunstfond [The State Foundation for the Arts] in 1989. "The Lady" first appeared in Hav's collection *Øjeblikket er en Åbning* [The Moment is an Opening] in 1983.

ASTRID SAALBACH (b. 1955) trained as an actor at the National Theatre School and she worked as a professional actor until a few years ago. Her debut as an author came in 1982 when she wrote the radio play, *Spor i sandet*

[Tracks in the Sand]. Since then she has written two more radio plays, two television dramas, three plays, of which one recently premiered at the Royal Theatre, a collection of short stories and in 1988 her novel *Den glemte skov* [The Forgotten Forest] was published. She has received several awards and prizes including the three-year award from Statens Kunstfond [the State Foundation for the Arts], Nordisk radiospilpris [The Nordic Price for Radio Drama], and Kjell Abell Prisen [the Kjell Abell Prize in playwriting.] "The Stain" was first published in the collection *Månens ansigt* [The Face of the Moon] in 1985.

CLAES JOHANSEN (b. 1957) made his debut at the age of seventeen in Gylendals Magasin. He then wrote for a music magazine and worked for Danish Radio. Nineteen-eighty-six saw the publication of his first collection of stories *Fyrgtelige Vera* [Terrible Vera] which was followed a year later by *De Sædvanlige Tragedier* [The Usual Tragedies]. In 1988 his first novel *Alt hvad der er muligt* [All that's Possible] appeared. "The little Newcomer" was first published in *Frygtelige Vera* in 1986. Claes Johansen re-worked the story in English for this collection.

HANNE MARIE SVENDSEN (b. 1933) has taught at the University of Copenhagen and worked as a producer at Danish Radio's department of theatre and literature. She has published three theoretical works on the Danish novel. She made her literary debut in 1977 with the novel *Mathildes Drømmebog* [Mathilde's Dream Book] and she has since published several novels and story collections. She has also written for the stage. Her novel *Guldkuglen* [The Gold Ball] from 1985 introduced her to American readers when it was published by Alfred A. Knopf in 1989. She has won several prizes and awards. "The Heights of Happiness" appeared in the story collection *Suset* published in tribute to Jytte Borberg in 1987.

SVEND ÅGE MADSEN (b. 1939) made his debut in 1963 with the novel Besøget [The Visit]. Since then he has published several books. He has written a great many plays for radio and the stage. He has travelled extensively in the U.S., Algeria, India and China. He has won several prizes including the Danish Dramatists' Prize of Distinction and the Jeppe [Danish Theatre's equivalent to the Tony.] "On the way to the Cemetery" first appeared in the anthology *At ønske en pludselig forvandling* [To Wish for a Sudden Change] in 1983.

DORRIT WILLUMSEN (b. 1940) specialized in the classical languages when she was in Gymnasium after which she was employed in an office, in a laboratory, a library and in a commercial gallery. She made her debut with the story collection *Knagen* [The Peg] in 1965. Since then she has published novels and short stories, in particular, but she has also written poetry, and drama for radio, the stage and television. In 1967 she received a three-year grant from Statens Kunstfond [The State Foundation for the Arts.] Her most well-known work is *Marie* (1983), a historical novel about Madame Tussaud. It has been translated into English, French, German, Norwegian, Swedish and Dutch. In 1981 she received Det Danske Akademi's [The Danish Academy] major literary prize. "To Wish for a Sudden Change" was first published anonymously in Luftskibet in 1982.